The Story of Simon

The Story of Simon

Rachel Loewen

Matador
9 Priory Business Park,
Wistow Road, Kibworth Beauchamp,
Leicestershire. LE8 0RX
Tel: 0116 279 2299
Email: books@troubador.co.uk
Web: www.troubador.co.uk/matador
Twitter: @matadorbooks

ISBN 978 1800460 393

British Library Cataloguing in Publication Data.
A catalogue record for this book is available from the British Library.

Printed and bound in the UK by TJ Books Limited, Padstow, Cornwall
Typeset in 11pt Minion Pro by Troubador Publishing Ltd, Leicester, UK

Matador is an imprint of Troubador Publishing Ltd

To those brave souls who leave behind the safe harbour of what they 'should' desire, and swim in the deeper waters.

One

Kate and Simon at the fetish ball

———

Kate waits in a corner of the room, watching the party. The music is blaring, the base line thumping. The bright lights flashing in the darkness overwhelm her senses, raising her excitement as she anticipates what the evening might hold.

She scans the room. The outfits are amazing – latex, leather, silk, feathers, spikes and chains. Everything from full period costume to body paint and piercings. Everyone has made an effort to look their best. The dress code is strictly enforced, of course, but people have gone above and beyond the minimum requirements.

She tugs at the hem of her mini skirt and straightens the straps of her top. She feels underdressed compared to the beautiful, artistically costumed people milling around her. Her feet are already aching in her high heels, but she is damned if she's going to sit down this early. Not before she's found a Dom to take her to the playroom.

Looking around she notices most people are here in pairs, come to play together. The ones who are alone are mostly submissives. There will be a lot of competition. Any Dominant who came alone will have their pick. Kate is determined she won't waste the ticket price on a night limited to drinking, dancing and watching others get led away to be tied up and whipped. Tonight she is going to find a play partner so she can go home sore, bruised and satisfied. The pain from her shoes is a promise of what is to come.

*

Simon picks his way through the crowd, trying not to spill the drinks. His leather trousers feel sticky and hot. The borrowed mesh top he wears makes him feel exposed, even though he is surrounded by people wearing much less. He isn't used to being shirtless and the material doesn't leave much to the imagination. His long blonde hair is tied back in a ponytail, but still sticks to his skin. He feels awkard here, out of place and out of his comfort zone. Attending a small town kink club was scant preparation for this festival of decadence.

Even attending that club had been a complete shock. It had been his first time at a BDSM event, and he'd spent the whole evening propping up a wall, keeping out of the way and trying not to stare at the bodies of the half-naked women being led around on leashes. Tonight he is a little less paralysed, but still overawed by his immersion in this exotic environment.

As he weaves across the room, he begins to notice more details. The skin-tight costumes, the platform shoes, the body jewellery, the extravagant makeup. The tight laced corsets and clothes with exaggerated projections, transforming their bearers with unnatural angles and sculpted curves. Not just the clothes but the accessories too; the collars and wrist cuffs, whips clipped to belts, the less-than-subtle hints at dominance and cruelty.

Threading through the crowd, he keeps his gaze low and tries not to bump into anyone. He still feels embarrassed being amongst these people. Embarrassed at the sight of so many individuals being open about their sexualities and their preferences for all things kinky. Not only open but proud, completely comfortable and unashamed about something which he has hidden for so long. Something he thought about in private, but never dared act out. At least, not in public. Not outside the secrecy of the bedroom, and only then after a lot of encouragement from his girlfriend. His now ex-girlfriend.

And that would have been the end of it, if Simon hadn't drunk too much one night and told Kate more than he should have done. Kate, who gleefully poured him another drink and plied him for more information about his relationship with his ex. Kate, who put him out of his misery by confessing that she, too, has a preference for a little sexual submission. Kate, who told him about the BDSM club scene, and who persuaded him to join her at Mistress Alannah's fetish ball. Kate, who arranged the tickets before worrying he might freak out, and insisted he "work up to it" by attending a regular club first.

That was two months ago. He would never have come to somewhere like this without Kate's encouragement. Hell, he would never have *known* about somewhere like this.

Tonight is in a different league from the first club. That had been friendly amateurs having fun together. This is more professional, with organised entertainment as well as the playroom and the bar. The night opened with a stage show. Simon loved watching Mistress Alannah perform. The fire breathing, the mesmerizing movements of the Dommes, the line of slaves being tortured for the crowd's entertainment. The Mistress herself commanding events with a whip in one hand and a flaming torch in the other, leading her cohort in subjecting their slaves to a range of painful and degrading punishments. He knew it was all choreographed of course; the special effects pre-planned and the slaves willing. But the pain was real. The submission was real. Watching it had cast a spell over him, like some kind of erotic hypnosis, stirring his imagination as much as his body. His soul soared to watch this strong and beautiful creature who demanded acts of worship from the lesser souls kneeling at her feet.

"Everyone's a little bit in love with Mistress Alannah," Kate laughed at him, "that's why they pay silly money for the privilege of serving as her slave."

Simon has never seen a pro Domme before. She certainly seemed terrifying. He tries to imagine what it would be like to visit her. Not that he would ever be that brave, let alone have the spare cash to afford her tribute rates.

No, he is happy hiding in the anonymity of the crowd, simply getting used to the idea that places like this exist. It is enough of a thrill just to be here, amongst the fetish players, watching and learning. Now the show is over, the audience is spreading out into the rest of the event space – drinking at the bar, filling the dance floor, pairing up and heading off together to make use of the bondage equipment provided in the infamous playroom.

Oh God, the playroom. Simon's stomach flips to think of it.

He peered into it on his way to the bar but didn't dare set foot inside. One glimpse of the whipping bench, the St Andrew's cross, and the array of whips and paddles had been enough to send him scurrying to get the drinks.

And yet... despite the fear, some part of him still wants to explore every last piece of equipment in that room. Such a strange feeling, the conflict between his desire to be tied down and controlled, and the fear of it really happening.

Perhaps, he admits to himself, he is most afraid that the reality will not match the fantasies he holds. What if it's disappointing? What if he can't take the pain? Or freaks out and makes a fool of himself, in front of the whole London scene?

Still, he would like to try it. In the right circumstance, with the right person. Just in case it is as wonderful, and as pleasurable, as he imagines. That's the real reason he allowed Kate to persuade him to come tonight. Allowed her to convince him he will not be disappointed, if only he can summon up the courage to speak out his shy desires and negotiate a scene. Kate should know, she's done it before, many times. She says it gets easier. She says that you just have to take the first step. It almost seems possible.

Yes, perhaps tonight he will be brave enough. Brave enough to let go and submit to someone. To allow them to tie him, and play with him, and do all those glorious things he'd glimpsed through the door of that playroom.

Two

Signing up for the Slave Auction

———

Simon squeezes past a final group of revellers and reaches Kate.

"Here you go, your vodka and coke. The bar prices are daylight robbery." He leans against the wall next to her, sipping his glass.

"Thanks," she replies. "So, are you ready yet? To look for someone to sub for? We could hang around the playroom and see if anyone likes the look of us?"

"I'm not sure – I still don't know if I can do it. I think I'll just stay here for a while, watch the crowd and work up my courage."

"Oh God Simon, you took long enough getting the drinks. I'm not waiting for you to work up your nerve. The later we leave it the more Doms will have picked subs to play with, and the less chance we'll have of finding someone. Man up, it's now or never! I'm not missing out on my best chance for a scene because you're dithering."

"OK, OK. Stop pressuring me, it's not helping." He frowns. "If you're so desperate for some action, why don't you sign up for the slave auction?"

"The what?" She tilts her head, eyes widening. "There's a slave auction? Oh wow! How come you know about that and I don't?"

"There was a poster by the bar. Slaves sign up and they're put on display in a cage. At midnight they're sold to the highest bidder for use on this night only. The money is going to some charity or other. The poster said it's guaranteed play, apparently if no-one buys you the house Doms will be forced to punish you for your shortcomings. They're taking volunteers in the stage room, where the show was."

He pauses, trying to gauge her reaction before continuing.

"Sounds like it's just what you're looking for? But you'd better go now, they're only signing slaves until the cage is full."

Kate is bouncing up and down in excitement.

"Simon, yes! It's perfect. Just perfect!" she gushes. Then she smiles, a mischievous look in her eyes.

"We can both sign up. It'll take all the awkwardness out of finding your first proper Mistress – you can let her choose you! It'll be a great introduction to the scene… And it's for charity so it'd be really bad to refuse, wouldn't it?"

She puts on her best pout and raises her eyebrows expectantly. Simon hesitates to respond.

"That's not what I meant. I don't think it's my sort of thing."

Kate continues her persuasion, fluttering her eyelashes. "Oh come on, say you will? It'll be great fun. And anyway, I can't exactly leave you on your own, can I? You'd have a terrible night. If you come too, we'll be in the slave cage together waiting to be sold. It'll be such a laugh. Go on Simon, it's time to take a deep breath and dive in. Do you really think you'll meet someone if I'm not on your case all night? You promised me that you wouldn't be a wallflower tonight. If you're going to stay on the margins you might as well just go home."

Simon sees she's not going to give up. He knows when Kate is determined she will keep asking and cajoling until she gets the answer she wants. Just like when she persuaded him to come here in the first place. Once she gets an idea into her head – once she decides she will make something happen – she just keeps going on and on about it until she gets her own way. He smiles. At times like this, when she stamps her foot and makes demands, he struggles to see her as the submissive she claims to be. Far too bossy. Maybe that's why he gave in and spent a small fortune on the ticket.

The trouble is, she's right. He will have a terrible night if she leaves him here alone. He will waste the evening standing by the wall and watching, just like he'd done at the first BDSM night. It had been the most thrilling night of his life, but he'd been too terrified to engage in any play. He'd promised himself the next time would be different. Well, tonight is the next time. And he doesn't want to wake up regretting an expensive waste of the door price.

Simon sighs, and downs his drink. "OK. OK, I'll do it. If only to shut you up."

*

Simon stands in front of a bored looking man in a military style PVC jacket and peaked cap.

"Right, you will be slave number ten and she'll be eleven. Write your names and details on these forms, describe the sort of play you like, anything you're not willing to try, and list any medical conditions we need to know about. We'll put them all together in our auction catalogue. Oh, and I need a picture of you too. Smile."

He lifts a Polaroid camera to his face. Simon looks into the lens but can't raise a smile. The flash is bright, sudden. It draws attention from a few bystanders. The square photo ejects from the bottom of the camera. Then it's Kate's turn. She is smiling, lowering her head and trying to look alluring. A second flash, another whirr as the camera ejects a second square of paper.

The auction clerk half-heartedly waves the pictures in the air whilst they develop. He checks they are acceptable – black and white head shots meant for photocopying into the catalogue book. When he is satisfied all is in order, he speaks again. "OK, that's it. Put your collars on and in you go. Oh, and make sure you go to the bathroom before we lock you in. You don't get out again until you're sold."

He hands Simon a shiny metal collar, lined with leather. It has a buckle fastening at the back and a D ring at the front. Hanging from the D ring is a dog tag with the number 10 engraved on it.

"Don't speak to the buyers unless you're spoken to, and keep your hands and feet to yourself. Mistress Julie is supervising the cage, so any trouble and you'll answer to her."

Simon feels his pulse quicken as he scans the stage and sees a woman in thigh high boots and a similar PVC uniform. He shakes his head and mutters "Oh shit, what am I doing?"

The clerk raises an eyebrow. "First time in the auction?"

Kate interrupts before Simon can get a word in. "It's his first time in the auction, and his first time playing any sort of scene. Unless you count one ex-girlfriend." She flashes a wide smile, proud that she persuaded Simon to join her.

"Ha!" laughs the clerk, a wry grin spreading over his face. "Brave man. Well, be sure to write THAT on the form. Should bring a bit of interest, it's not every auction we have a virgin to sell."

Simon looks from the clerk to Kate and back again, wondering if it's too late to back out.

It is.

*

He fastens the collar around his neck and crawls into the cage. Kate follows him, wittering on about something or other, looking very pleased with herself. Simon is not really listening. The cage is long and narrow, set up at the front of the stage, above the main floor level. Already it is half full of people. The space is low, too low to stand up inside. He can't even kneel upright; he is forced to remain on all fours. The stage lights are shining down on him, and suddenly he feels hot again, flushed with sweat and anticipation. He looks out at the handful of men and women milling around the room.

"Any one of these," he thinks. "It could be any one of them. Someone will buy me, and tie me up, and do whatever they like to me." His ears thud with the sound of his heartbeat, and he begins to feel sick.

"What the hell am I doing?" he whispers under his breath. "How the hell did I let you talk me into this?" But despite the nerves, somewhere in the middle of his being there is a growing calm. A part of him that has already relinquished control. A part that has trusted his safety, even his very life, to another, to someone more powerful than himself. All responsibility has already lifted from his shoulders, and all he needs to do is obey. There is a deep peace about the idea.

He glances at Kate. She is watching his expression, gazing at him with a look somewhere between satisfaction and concern.

"Enjoying yourself yet?"

Three

The bidders gather

Half an hour later, Simon is beginning to relax. Every
time he thinks of the auction ahead he feels a shooting
panic, rising from his stomach up to his throat. He tries
not to dwell on it. Instead he concentrates on watching the
people in the room; observing the Masters and Mistresses
as they chat to each other, glance towards the cage, and
occasionally come over for a closer look at the people for
sale. Many seem to know each other. They embrace like
old friends, or else have animated conversations about
goodness knows what. A woman in a black corset holding
a Venetian mask whispers something – a joke perhaps, or
a secret – to her friend. They burst out laughing and turn
to look at a man across the room. Her friend opens her
fan and covers her face to hide her giggles. The man sees
them, blushes, and makes a hasty exit.

Small interactions, windows on other people's games,

these keep Simon's mind distracted, stopping him from dwelling on the coming auction and what might happen to him after it.

Oh God, what will happen to him? He takes a deep breath, then exhales slowly. Time ticks on.

*

The other slaves in the cage are snatching whispered conversations. They are not supposed to talk to each other, at least Mistress Julie tells them off when she catches them. But Kate, crouching on his left, still manages to chat with the slave next to her. The girl to Simon's right is more circumspect, she gives him a quick nod of acknowledgement, a smile, then looks away. She does not attempt to speak to him. Simon studies the tattoo on her shoulder, an intricately drawn plant creeping from her back down to her arm, almost to the elbow. It has little pink flowers amongst the green leaves and winding stems. Next to the central stem there is a word – he tries to read it but he cannot make it out.

Simon's attention is drawn back to the room outside the cage, to a growing queue of people outside a door at the far end of the room. Another uniformed staff member stands between the queue and the door. She is talking to the man at the front, who is middle aged and overweight. His paunch spills over the top of a shiny latex skirt, his only item of clothing. The guard is writing notes on a clipboard. She disappears through the door, shutting it behind her. The man fidgets, shuffling his feet. A few minutes later she reappears. A short conversation, she shakes her head. The man turns and walks away, he looks disappointed. The guard starts talking to the next person in the line.

The door swings open again. This time a tall woman with a punk hairstyle emerges. She is topless, clutching a piece of clothing across her chest to cover her breasts. She carries a bra in one hand. Despite her state of undress, her expression is serene as she glides across the room, lost in her own thoughts. She disappears into the bathroom. As she turns the corner, Simon sees a large rectangle of white gauze taped to the back of her shoulder. As the light emanating from the bathroom engulfs her, he sees a trail of drying blood snaking down her back.

*

"Kate?" Simon whispers. He keeps his eyes on the door at the far end of the room, not daring to turn towards her in case Mistress Julie is watching. More forcefully; "Kate?"

"What? Are you OK? Hey, this girl next to me was a slave in the stage show last year, isn't that cool?" Kate is still hyperactive, buzzing on the adrenaline. Not even being locked in a slave cage can shut her up.

"Kate, what's behind that door over there? What are those people waiting for?"

"What door? Where?"

"Over there, on the other side of the room? That metal door with the queue of people. What's going on inside?"

"Oh, that. That's Mistress Alannah's private playroom. Invite only. They're trying to get in. Waste of time, you queue for ages and they turn most people away."

Simon thinks for a minute, not sure if he is any the wiser. "So what happens inside?"

"Silence!"

Simon jumps, as Mistress Julie's riding crop clangs down onto the roof of the cage, just above his head.

"If you two don't shut up I will drag you out of that cage and make you shut up."

"Yes Mistress. Sorry Mistress." Kate says, almost singing the words. She is smiling, enjoying the game.

Simon isn't smiling. The panic is shooting up from his stomach again. Suddenly, it all feels very real.

*

As midnight approaches, the crowd thickens. Dominants interested in bidding, submissives just watching, a host of cross dressed and half dressed kinksters here to witness the next instalment of the evening's entertainment. These people are the serious players. Their dress is less costume and more functional fetish than the average attendee. They are not here to observe, but to partake.

Activity around the cage increases. Those considering making a purchase inspect the slaves more closely. Each bidder holds a thin bundle of papers in their hand – the catalogue. Many ask questions, demanding clarification of what each slave has written on their sign in sheet. The questions Simon overhears do nothing to salve his nerves.

"Do you mind being marked?"

"Have you brought your own clamps?"

"How much weight can you bear on those piercings?"

Simon avoids eye contact, but can't help stealing glances at the Mistresses who pause to examine him. In ten minutes time, one of them will be leading him away into the play room. Another rush of adrenaline. Another thrill as he imagines himself bound, powerless, but perversely safe under another's control.

Once again he attempts to still his racing mind with deep breaths. It is getting harder as the auction approaches. Even Kate is subdued now, her excitement giving way to nerves.

She reaches over and gives his hand a squeeze, letting go quickly before she is spotted.

"I'm OK," he whispers back. "Don't worry, I think I'm OK."

*

A sudden quietening, then a rapid murmur of gossip, ripples through the room. The source of the commotion is at the far end of the cage to his right, just out of Simon's view. He cranes to see what the others stare at. Every eye in the room is focussed on… what?

Finally he sees. A man, a solitary figure paces slowly down the line of caged slaves. Long black hair, tied at the nape. The man wears a black shirt, open at the neck. Plain black jeans. He does not seem to fit with the elaborately attired crowd. Only a length of rope hanging from his belt identifies him as part of the scene. But something in the way he carries himself, something in his steadiness leaves no doubt of his authority. Deliberately, the man turns the pages of the catalogue, examining each slave in turn. He says nothing, asks nothing. His silence seems to add to his aura of power. He has no need for further information, no desire for knowledge beyond his possession.

The man draws closer. Wondering who he is, Simon drops his head low and stares at the floor, hoping to be ignored and passed over.

Out of the corner of his eye, Simon sees the girl on his right tense up, and lower her head too. He waits, straining to hear footsteps passing by, but the background noise of the room is too loud.

He glances up.

In shock, he realises too late that his timing is exactly wrong. The Master is right next to him, close enough to touch. Simon's gaze locks on his piercing blue eyes, and is trapped there for a heart stopping moment, before finally he is able to break free, to look down, to breathe again. The Master moves on.

Simon squeezes his eyes tightly shut, doubling his efforts to slow his shallow breaths. He steals a glance at Kate. Happy go lucky Kate. Giggling, excitable Kate, to whom everything is just a bit of fun. Unbelievably, she looks shaken too.

The Master reaches the end of the cage and gestures to Mistress Julie, who immediately walks over to him. They talk, ignoring the raised eyebrows of the people around them.

*

"Who the fuck is that?" Simon whispers, confident that Julie is too busy to notice.

"Oh. My. God." Kate exclaims, forgetting to whisper. "That is Master Richard. Holy crap. He can't be...?" she turns to the slave on her left. "He isn't buying, right?" The slave just shrugs and shakes her head.

"What's going on? Why is everyone so worked up?" Simon asks.

Kate sighs, regaining some of her composure. On safe ground again as Simon's educator, she explains.

"They're freaked out because he's basically this major sadist. He's one of the house Doms at Club Pain but he's pretty extreme even for them. He's got his own dungeon at home where he sees private clients. They say he's got full time live-in slaves. And... Simon, the stuff he's known for... well, it's stuff that most Doms won't do. Stuff that's in the legal grey zone. You know, things that can get you arrested if you're not very careful."

Having shared her gossip, her tone changes as her thoughts return to the auction and to what Master Richard's presence might mean for her. She continues, less sure of herself.

"Why would a man like that want to buy a slave? He's got a queue of people waiting to pay him for it? He's just come to have a look, right? To scare us? He wouldn't... actually... bid?" Kate trails off, her face sombre.

"I reckon a guy like that might do anything he damn well liked." Simon teases. He is only half joking.

"Oh, great, thanks for the support." She snaps, angrily. "Well don't think you're safe just because you're a bloke."

Simon's eyes widen. "You mean... he's not... he's not into men too?" He pauses, brow furrowed.

"He sees male subs, yes. Maybe he's more interested in whether you're an obedient slave than whether you're male or female. Either way he scares the shit out of me."

"Seriously, Kate, this auction is supposed to be fun, right? Supposed to be based on consent? So – what happens if I want to bail out? What if I can't go through with it?"

"I don't know for sure. I guess they'd have to let you walk away. You might get blacklisted from future events." Something occurs to her, and her eyes twinkle with mischief. "But Simon – isn't that what the forms are for? You were supposed to write down what you want, and what you're not willing to try. I mean, did you put on your form that you don't want any violent anal rape from a professional sadist?"

Simon splutters, shakes his head, then grins back. "Did you?"

Kate sniggers, breaking the tension. Simon can't be spiralling into panic if he can still joke about it. Luckily, Mistress Julie is still out of earshot.

"We're going to be fine, Simon, just fine. Master Richard won't be interested in the likes of us. We're not hard core enough for him. You're right, this is supposed to be a blast, just a bit of fun. Let's stop worrying and try to enjoy ourselves. Anyway it's too late now, looks like they're starting." She nods in the direction of the uniformed clerk who signed them up. He is gathering his papers together and waving at the PA desk.

"Oh God, Kate, what the hell have you talked me into?"

"Only the best night of your entire life Simon, and you can thank me later."

There is no time to reply, as Mistress Julie returns with a microphone in her hand. A spotlight focusses on her, the room lights dim, and the auction begins.

.

Four

Richard decides to buy a slave

———

30 MINUTES EARLIER

Richard watches the scenes unfolding in the playroom. Three stairs rise from the room to a fire exit, his favourite vantage point in this venue. At his feet, Sarah sits heavily on the lowest step, her leash hanging in a steep arc across his body to the handle looped around his wrist. She is not permitted to lean against him, but she is close. So close, he can feel her breathing, the familiar motion of his favourite slave inhaling and exhaling.

He knows she wants to be taken to the bench. She hopes to be restrained, beaten, to have the screams coaxed out of her. He knows how much she enjoys being shown off in public. She takes pride in her ability to endure all that he demands, to be known as one of the few slaves good enough to please him.

He will not satisfy her tonight. He has other things on his mind.

Like his wife.

He considers his plan one last time. He knows he should apologise. He acted unreasonably, blaming her for something which she had not done deliberately. Worse, he has been brooding since he heard the news, remaining angry while the reality of their altered situation sank in.

Now he is ready to talk about it. It is his responsibility to take the first step. God knows, she tolerates enough for him. There aren't many women who would accept his lifestyle, let alone embrace it.

That is the problem, he thinks. There is no rule book for this. Romantic relationships in the BDSM world are almost all Dom / sub. There are few precedents for a Dom / Domme couple, and no template on how to admit error for those who spend their lives ordering others around. With a slave, of course, there is never any need to back down. It would be positively counter-productive. Better to punish the slave for invoking the error. Especially if it is not their fault.

With his wife it is altogether different. He loves her, but more than that, he respects her. And he has treated her unjustly. She's been working so hard recently, and he knows his remoteness has made that more difficult. She has not asked his opinion on her ideas, as she usually would. These past few days she has stayed out of his way entirely. Waiting for him to calm down and realise he has been an idiot. Waiting for the inevitable apology, something which he is far from used to offering.

He sighs. She knew he would reach this point, from the moment they argued. Without a word she had sized up the situation and divined the best way to deal with it. She always seems to understand what others are thinking, and how best to manipulate them. It is why she is so good at what she does, and why she saw beyond his reputation to the man beneath.

In the vanilla world he might have bought her flowers, or chocolates, but that is not their culture. He will buy a gift worthy of her.

Recently she complained of a growing frustration with her work. Part of a more general fatigue, perhaps. She was sick and tired, she said, of pandering to her clients' fetishes whilst never finding the opportunity to explore her own. One of the perils of being a pro, of course. But she could do with a change. She might appreciate having someone who is not paying for a service but is there for her pleasure alone.

Yes, his plan is sound. Providing it is permitted to buy a slave for someone else. He will check with the auction mistress.

It will have to be the right slave though. Long hair, of course. But the right demeanour too. Someone who is not too jaded. They should not ruin her mood with disappointment if she chooses a mild scene. Yes, someone whose expectations are not too high. He will have to choose carefully.

Good, it is decided.

Briskly, he stoops down and unzips the kit bag on the floor. His hand rummages in the depths, then emerges clutching an object wrapped in black tissue paper, tied with a red bow. It is 9 inches long, a flat shape, broader than it is deep. Sliding it into his back pocket, he reaches into the bag again and pulls out a length of rope.

He secures the rope to his belt and turns to address Sarah. She looks up expectantly, believing her opportunity to prove her devotion has come. Wrong.

He barks his order. "Stay here. Look after the bag. Don't speak to anyone, don't play with anyone. Understood?"

Hurt fills her eyes. She swallows down her disappointment. "Yes, Master."

Richard smiles. She is beautiful like that. Upset, unfulfilled, and desperately supressing her emotions in an effort to please him. He will remember those sad eyes later, when he has her alone, tied and exposed in his private dungeon. He will recall the tremble of her bottom lip as she submits her desires to his. He feels himself growing hard, and checks his thoughts. Later. More of that later.

First, he must put things right with his wife.

"Good girl. I will be back within the hour. I expect you to be waiting for me, and ready to leave."

"Yes Master."

He discards her leash and strides out of the door, toward the stage room.

*

Richard looks around the stage room, noticing a number of acquaintances, regular attendees from Club Pain who are amongst the more dedicated players in the city. Alongside them, the shy newcomers. Part time perverts looking to condense a month's desire into one night's play. Voyeurs getting kicks watching the engrossed players or ogling the half dressed. And the hangers on, the ones who are present merely for the titillation of revealing their experiences to friends in hushed tones over dinner. Richard has no time for such parasites.

Circling around the outside of the room, he reaches the far end of the cage. He picks up a catalogue from the badly photocopied pile lying on a side table. Briefly flicking through the pictures in the booklet, he is pleased to realise he does not recognise any of the faces. Aside from parasitic hangers on, there is little he finds more annoying than an experienced slave who's gone too long without a scene and is in the grip of the frenzy – needy and desperate for any sort of domination they can get. Richard holds little sympathy for them – too rebellious to please a Master and too poor to pay for one.

He counts the slaves on offer – fifteen in all. The cage imprisoning them is low and narrow. Far too small for their number. He smiles, imagining what his wife would say. Something about the fire hazard or conditions attached to the public liability insurance. No matter, it is too late to concern her with it now. The slaves kneel in a disorganised row, down on all fours and facing into the room.

Richard returns his attention to the beginning of the catalogue, and starts to read.

The first slave wants bondage play, ideally Japanese rope. A possible. Richard approaches the cage, looking down his nose at the nearest crouching supplicant. She has short spiky hair. No good.

The second slave is a foot worshipper, boring, no good.

The third enjoys humiliation and enforced feminisation, no good.

The fourth is very specific about the types of torture he prefers. Richard runs his eyes over the caged man in front of him. Well built, muscled even. Dressed in latex. His hair is long and curly. A possible. Certainly the physical elements are a fit, but the specific nature of his preferences imply he is an old hand – which is a distinct drawback.

The fifth, sixth, seventh – all no good. Eight is better, a Chinese girl whose hair falls to the floor. Her sign up sheet explains that she enjoys tight lacing, and the sensation of silk on skin. Yes, this one is the best so far.

Number nine has nothing to recommend her as unique or particularly interesting.

Number ten… Richard skims the words on the page… one line stands out.

"First timer, looking for an experienced Mistress to show me what this is all about."

Promising. If it's true, which is unlikely. Why would such an inexperienced slave sign up for the auction?

Richard raises his eyes to inspect the man in front of him. The slave's clothing is simple, a mesh top and leather trousers. Just enough to meet the dress code, plausible clothing for someone new to the scene. His head is bowed, hung low. He has long blonde hair, straight, tied at the back of his head in a band.

Very promising.

Without warning, the slave looks up, looks directly at him. Richard watches as his expression changes from confusion, to shock, to blind panic. His pupils dilate wildly.

Richard holds his gaze, entranced. Seeing the slave's obvious terror inflames a hunger to possess him, to break him. Delicious imaginings about what he might do to someone so naïve, so completely unguarded.

A second later, maybe two, the slave regains control of his eyes, and looks down. The spell is broken.

Yes, this is the one. This is definitely the one.

Perhaps after his wife is finished with him, Richard might conduct a scene too.

Stepping forward, Richard glances at the eleventh page in the catalogue, then the twelfth. Confident of his choice, he closes the booklet. As he reaches the end of the cage he beckons the auction mistress, towards him.

"Your name?"

"Mistress Julie. Will you be bidding in tonight's auction, Master Richard?"

"Perhaps. First I have a question to ask you."

"Of course, what is it?"

"Is it permitted to purchase a slave as a gift for someone else to play with?"

Julie's expression gives away her surprise.

"Umm… well it's not usual. But no, I don't think there is a rule against it. It would be your risk if the recipient was unwilling to use the slave. We do have a guaranteed play policy."

"That would not be a concern for me."

"Oh, OK, fine. Then yes, it's permitted. May I ask who you are buying for?"

Richard raises one eyebrow, hiding his embarrassment by pursing his lips.

"Who do you think?"

Julie's face softens. "Oh, yes, of course. How romantic."

Richard scowls.

"Thank you Mistress Julie, that will be all."

He dismisses her as casually as he summoned her. Hastily, he stalks away, into the centre of the room.

A minute later, the room lights dim, and the auction begins.

Five

Sold

———

Mistress Julie stands in the spotlight, microphone in one hand and auction catalogue in the other.

"Good evening ladies and gentlemen, Doms and subs, perverts and pleasure seekers and all the kinky people in between. Welcome to the next diversion of the evening, for your entertainment and amusement – the slave auction!"

The room erupts in a cheer.

"Thank you, thank you, I know you are all eager to see who will win the bidding for our fifteen pieces of fresh meat."

Another cheer. The crowd is in high spirits, expectant about the ritual to come.

"Remember, ladies and gentlemen, it's all for a good cause so dig deep and bid high. Just a reminder to any new customers that your slave's price must be paid immediately in full before you can collect your purchase, we take cash and credit cards. The buyer is responsible for gaining consent for any scenes. You should not assume that anything written in the auction catalogue constitutes consent. This house believes that the best kind of play is safe play. We recommend the use of a safe word especially when playing scenes with a stranger. If you would like any guidance on keeping it safe sane and consensual, help on how to use the equipment, or any other technical tips from the pros, then please speak to someone in a uniform like mine."

"That's the legal bit covered. We seem to have a good turn out, and I can see you are all raring to go, so I will get straight to business and open the first lot."

"Slave number one enjoys bondage and is hoping for a little Japanese rope play. Shibari is a beautiful art, and if you haven't brought your own rope we do provide it in the playroom. I'll start the bidding at £10."

Several people bid and the price rises over £100 before Mistress Julie calls sold. The buyer steps out of the crowd and approaches the desk, where the auction clerk now sits next to a cash box and a credit card machine. Price paid, the buyer climbs the stairs to the stage.

Meanwhile, Mistress Julie opens the cage door and helps slave one to her feet. After so long in a confined space, the slave is stiff and cannot stand easily. She leans on the Mistress' arm to steady herself. Her buyer approaches, and she smiles like Christmas morning when he produces a length of beautiful red silk rope. He threads it through the D ring on her collar, and leads her off the stage.

Mistress Julie lifts her microphone to her lips.

"I think we have our first happy customers. And who would have guessed it would be Kieran? I don't believe I've ever seen that man with less than 60 feet of rope on him. I think they're going to have a lot of fun, don't you?"

Cheers, and applause from the crowd.

"Our second lot is a foot fan, he prefers naked feet but is also happy with shoes and boots. If anyone is regretting the height of their heels tonight, this is your chance to take them off and get a good foot massage. Now, who will start me at £10?"

*

The auction progresses slowly. As the cage empties, Simon and Kate have more room to move. They spread out, drifting closer and closer to Mistress Julie's cage door. Slave after slave is sold, some fetching a higher price than others. Before long, slave nine is being auctioned, being helped out of the cage, having a chain clipped to her collar. She descends the stairs with her new owner.

Simon's turn.

"Good luck," Kate whispers, as Simon's number is announced. "If I don't catch up with you later I'll meet you at the cloakroom at closing time, OK?"

Simon nods. Closing time. Three a.m. Two hours, forty minutes, and a whole lifetime away. He is so full of conflicting emotions that his mind cannot focus on any single thought for long. When he tries to concentrate each idea melts, running away from him like mercury. He flits from hope to fear, desire to trepidation. It is too late to escape now, it was too late an hour ago. He has climbed on to the roller coaster and now he must ride it out.

*

Julie begins. "Next we have slave number ten. Ladies and gentlemen, slave number ten is a very special lot because this poor soul is a play virgin. Yes, that's right, he's fresh and keen and new to the scene, and he's looking for an experienced Mistress to show him what we're all here for!"

The crowd cheers.

"From the look on his face I think he's regretting it now, but he signed the form and we're going to sell him whether he likes it or not!"

More cheers, and a wolf whistle from the back of the room.

"I think you'll agree this one is worth a bit of a premium. So who will start me off at £50?"

Simon's eyes dart around the room as he looks for movement – who will raise their hand, who will bid for him?

Relief, as a pretty young woman in a purple corset raises her hand.

"Very good, and do I see £75? £75 anywhere? Yes, you at the side, I have £75."

This time it is a mature women, perhaps 40, with short hair gelled back from her face. Not unattractive, if a little severe looking.

"And £100? Who will give me £100 for a brand new pet?"

A hand is raised in the centre of the room. Simon strains to look, but the figure is too deep in the crowd. Kate shifts her weight too, trying to peer through the heads. Neither can see.

"Thank you, we have a third bidder, in the middle towards the back." Julie nods toward the hand, then surveys the crowd with a smile, announcing, "This could be an interesting one ladies and gentlemen."

As Julie speaks, the crowd follows the direction of her nod, turning to discover the identity of the third bidder. From those nearest come whispers, then nervous laughter. As others turn to see, the crowd moves, and a gap opens revealing the third bidder. It is Master Richard.

Freefall.

Simon's mind is in freefall, plummeting down into blackness. "Oh God, no. Oh please God, no," is all he can speak.

Kate is panicking too. "Shit. Shit shit shit." Her face is a portrait of horror.

"Do I see £125? Will anyone give me £125?"

A short reprieve as the woman in the purple corset bids again. Ended quickly by another bid from Master Richard.

"£175?" Julie scans the room, looking for any new bidders. None volunteer themselves.

The severe looking woman makes one more bid, then bows out.

It is a two way fight, backwards and forwards between the purple corseted woman and the Master. The price rises and rises.

Simon watches the woman, this potential saviour, his eyes pleading with her. At every bid he prays that she continues, prays that she has mercy on him. She glances towards him, gives a coquettish smile, and raises her hand one more time. £325.

Richard bids immediately and without hesitation. £350.

The woman looks at Simon again, and hesitates.

"Please. Please keep going. Please rescue me." he wills. He prays it so hard he is sure she must feel it. She must keep going. She must.

She raises her hand. £375. Relief.

£400. No hesitation. No wavering. No hope.

The woman shakes her head, smiles and shrugs, admitting defeat. Master Richard has won.

"Sold, to the man in black. A new auction record I think – and may God have mercy on your soul!"

Even the crowd is too surprised to cheer.

*

Simon cannot feel his arms or legs as the cage door opens, and Mistress Julie takes his hand to lead him out towards the danger beyond. The room feels distant, the sounds are far off. This body is not his own. It is alien to him, irrelevant. He feels untethered, adrift. He is soaring high above, out of reach. Everything moves slowly, a pantomime dance of Julie's hand, and standing up, and those piercing blue eyes weaving through the crowd towards him.

Then bang, he is back in the heat and the noise and the

smell of his own sweat. Palpitations in his chest, he cannot breathe, he is going to die.

A voice from the cage behind him – Kate. "I'm so sorry Simon. I didn't mean for it to be like this. Your first time… I'm so sorry."

*

Mistress Julie takes pity on him as they wait for Richard to pay. "Keep breathing slave. Try not to panic. Look at me. LOOK at me. It's not how it seems. Don't bail out until you know what's going on and you're sure you want out. Understand?" Her concern feels maternal, protective. He clings to her arm.

Master Richard walks up the stairs, inexorably nearer and nearer. He draws a length of rope from his belt, folds it in two.

Paralyzed, Simon watches as the loop of rope in the Master's hand glides towards his throat. At the very last moment his instincts kick in, he pulls back, leaning away from his captor. A futile gesture of escape.

Master Richard narrows his eyes, steps forward and thrusts the loop through the D ring on Simon's collar. Feeding the loose ends through the loop, he pulls it tight. The rope snaps into a taught line from the collar to the Master's grip.

Trapped.

Richard utters one word, then turns on his heels and walks off the stage.

"Come."

Six

Claimed

———

Richard sets a quick pace through the stage room and into the bar beyond. The slave behind him struggles to keep up. Richard winds the rope around his fist, gripping tight.

Flighty, he thinks. This slave is flighty. That ridiculous attempt to dodge the leash. And his breathing, uncontrolled and fast like a panting dog. Flighty, and at risk of tripping out.

The first thing that must be done is to calm him down.

A fast walk will burn off some of the adrenaline. Get him out of the immediate location, give him a chance to realise nothing has happened to him. Yet.

Richard smiles. At least a spectacle like that will do wonders for his reputation. Those shocked gasps from the crowd. That stunned silence as he won the bidding. So much of the art of control is in the illusion, in building the fear of what you might do, rather than what you are doing.

True, he plays a little harder than most, and does not shy away from the darker scenes. But he is very careful of the foundations – consent, honesty, his responsibility for the welfare of his submissives. For their enjoyment within the control he exerts. It is his reputation which encourages their fear, and that fear deepens his power. It rarely serves him to allow anyone to see past the image he projects to the real person behind. To the person with regrets and vulnerabilities like any other. The person about to apologise to his wife in front of a room full of her employees.

That's if he can calm this damn slave down. Once a submissive's mind has given in to terror it is not easy to coax it back into equilibrium. There is a risk he will remain flighty all night, too defensive to trust, too terrified to yield sufficiently to enjoy playing a scene.

This could turn into an expensive lack of apology.

*

Richard reaches the bar. He turns to face the slave.

"Stop."

Simon is confused. Why have they stopped here, half way to the playroom? What has he done wrong? Can he use this chance to escape, to unbuckle the collar, slip it off and get the hell out?

The Master's voice: "Do you drink alcohol?"

More confusion. He's buying me a drink? Like some kind of twisted date? This isn't what he expected at all. It's… bizarre. Surreal. He must have misunderstood.

The Master watches him, waiting for an answer. Tentatively, Simon nods.

Richard orders a large vodka, and sets it on the bar in front of Simon.

"Drink this. All of it."

Simon picks up the glass, suspicious. He downs the liquid in one, two gulps. It is strong. Caustic. It burns down past his throat and settles warmly in his stomach.

"Good. That will take the edge off your fear. You need to calm down. I'm not going to hurt you. I'm not going to do anything to you without your agreement. Do you understand?"

Simon nods.

"Do you believe me?"

Simon stares at the floor. By the smallest degree, he shakes his head.

The Master laughs.

"Well at least you're honest. Now, stand up straight, lift your head and let me look at what I have bought."

Reluctantly, Simon straightens up and raises his chin. He picks a spot across the room and stares at it.

The Master slowly circles around him, first one way, then the other. Simon is inspected from head to toe, up and down and up again. It seems to take a long time. Simon wonders what this man is thinking, what could he be plotting? Is he pleased with me? Do I want him to be? All the while, the Master holds firmly to the rope leash.

Simon feels the alcohol percolating into his bloodstream, feels it begin to make the edges of his world blurry. He remembers and regrets the drink he had with

Kate before the auction. Dutch courage, she'd said. Kate, who promised him it would all be fine. Kate, who would be sold herself by now, presumably somewhere in the building serving her new Master. Or Mistress. Simon wonders if she is pleased with her buyer or if she, too, feels like she's been bought by the devil himself.

"Good, you will suffice. Now tell me, why are you so upset that I bought you?"

Simon flushes. He remembers Kate describing him as a major sadist, known for playing scenes that could get the police called. Simon recalls her fear, which ignited his. He thinks of the joke she made about the sign in sheet. Oh God, he can't say that. How can he explain? What should he say to minimise the risk of angering him? Or worse, to speak something which may be received as a suggestion. He cannot risk provoking this man into doing exactly what he fears.

After a moment Simon settles on an idea.

"It's just that… that I was expecting to serve a Mistress. I didn't think a Master would buy me."

Richard knows there is more to the slave's fear than this, but does not push further. It appears the slave has some common sense after all. Richard speaks gently, pleased at the slave's response and careful not to scare him further.

"Well, you shall serve a Mistress tonight, if all goes according to my plan. I did not buy you for myself, slave. You are a gift."

A gift? A gift to a Mistress? Simon's mind churns. Is it true, or just a cruel game?

If it is true then he is safe… safe from this man at least.

Relief drenches him, flowing through his veins with the alcohol, warming his extremities.

"One question then, slave. I will permit you one choice, and only because the auction rules are very specific about guaranteed play. Do you consent to be a gift and to serve the Mistress I have bought you for? She does not know of my intention, and may refuse you." Richard brings his face closer to the slave, so they are eye to eye. "Or shall I take you to the playroom myself, where I guarantee you will receive my attention?"

The thought of following Master Richard into a room full of bondage equipment is enough to give Simon his voice back.

"Yes, Sir. I will. I consent to serve her."

"Good. Then it is decided."

Richard sighs. He contemplates the implied insult in the slave's decision: that any unknown Mistress is preferable to serving him. He decides to count it as a compliment instead, an act of obedience fuelled by fear. His plan is working, and that is all he cares about tonight. He gives a gentle tug on the rope.

"Come."

*

Richard leads the slave away from the bar, back into the stage room.

Simon is perplexed by their route, until they stop at the door to the bathroom. Richard lets go of the rope, and gestures towards the door.

"Two minutes only. Don't keep me waiting."

"Yes, Sir." Satisfied that the Master shows no signs of following him, Simon rushes through the door, finds a urinal and relieves himself.

A moment of reflection. He is still alive. He may even have escaped the clutches of Master Richard. And he is going to serve a Mistress. Things are definitely improving. Maybe he can cope with this after all. He allows himself to speculate: Who will she be? What will she look like? And what will she do with him? A flicker of excitement. Yes, it has been a terrifying start but things are definitely looking up.

Drying his hands, Simon exits the bathroom. Wordlessly, the Master takes up the rope leash and walks off. Simon trails close behind, allowing anticipation to tingle upward through his chest. He is being led towards a Mistress. To his Mistress. To the possibility of his fantasies becoming real.

He is not paying attention to where they are going. He does not notice until they pause at the door. The metal door in the far corner of the stage room, with the queue of people hoping to be admitted. The Master leads him past the queue, right to the door itself.

The guard looks up from her clipboard, and startles.

"Master Richard! We watched the auction... we thought that..." She looks from Richard, to Simon, and back again, then begins again with an awkward smile. "We weren't expecting you yet."

"Well here I am. As you can see. Are you going to let me in?" He looks expectantly at her.

"Of course." Hastily, she fumbles to open the door.

It swings towards them. Music is playing beyond, a different track to the one in the public space behind them. The air beyond has a floral scent – roses and jasmine. And something else too… another sort of outdoor summer smell. Something familiar, but out of place. Simon's brain delivers the answer a beat later. Barbeque. Burnt meat.

Oh God, burnt flesh.

A voice, a woman's voice, counts slowly. "Five. Six. Seven." Between each number, a loud crack, and a moan of pain.

The rope tugs on his collar, and Simon is led through the metal door into the room beyond.

Seven

The Handover

Richard steps through the door into Alannah's private playroom, leading the slave behind him. His annoyance at the door guard's hesitation evaporates as he catches sight of his wife.

She is engrossed in a scene with a musclebound male slave. She still wears her stage outfit – a black and red corset decorated in flame patterns, long black gloves, a short A-line skirt and knee length boots with deadly heels. She is punishing the slave with a bullwhip, its tail dipped in spirits and set alight. With every lash the flames stream out from the flying tip. The crack of each strike on the slave's back leaves a blackened burn around the fine red welt. A difficult scene which requires her full concentration. He will not distract her by approaching.

Alannah stands alone, her assistants keeping well away from the reach of the backlash. Her hair is held back from her face, cascading in waves down her back. It reflects the light from the flames. Her figure, all soft curves and taut muscle, is shown off to perfection as she flicks her arm behind the weight of the whip.

Beautiful, Richard thinks, allowing himself an appreciative sigh. Strong and powerful. One of the few people he holds worthy of his respect and trust. The only one of his lovers he does not play power games with. The only one who is his equal. For a moment, all he wants is to bury his face in her hair, wrap himself around her and lay together in the privacy of their room, the closed door hiding them from everything which is not simply her and him. How foolish he'd been to get angry with her. It was his fault, his raw nerve which was touched, triggering a reflex of aggression. He should not have allowed himself to blame her. The weakness was his alone. No matter, he will make amends, and they will move past it. He will begin by apologising for his behaviour.

Alannah counts slowly with each flick of the whip.

"Eight." The slave arches in pain, crying out with a low moan. The whip leaves a brief line of flame on his flesh, cauterising the welt.

"Nine." The strike is harder this time, leaving more burning spirit on the flesh. The flames sit there for a second or two as the slave twists in pain.

*

Richard's nostrils fill with the smell of burning skin. Mmmh, that smell, so evocative. He closes his eyes and remembers the last time he savoured it. Danny.

It was the day Danny signed the contract to become his full time slave. To mark the occasion, Richard had branded his precious boy, given him a permanent mark to show who owned him. The branding disc had been red hot, glowing on the end of the iron. And Danny, always vocal, had shouted and screamed as his flesh burned, writhing so much that he tore open the skin of his wrist against his restraints. Afterwards, with the disc taken off, he lay there shivering and sobbing, whispering his thanks over and over to his Master for claiming him. Promising that he would always serve him and always obey. Hearing Danny's pitiful cries, seeing the depths of his brokenness and unfettered submission, Richard had been consumed by a lust to possess him even more deeply, to own every last part of him. He should have stopped and seen to the wounds but instead he ripped at Danny's clothes and took what he wanted. Ignoring those responsibilities had been part of the pleasure, knowing that Danny was entirely his to use however and whenever he wanted, starting at that very moment, strapped to the table with his trousers round his ankles, his new brand still smouldering, getting fucked whilst he bled and whimpered, and all the while repeating his whispered vow of obedience.

Aah, Danny.

Richard smiles, and opens his eyes.

*

Alannah swings her arm and arcs the bullwhip one last time.

"Ten." The whip slices into the slave, eliciting a final cry. Alannah drops the flaming leather into a bucket of water, quenching the fire. The narrow focus of her concentration broadens, and she steps back to survey her work. Satisfied, she praises the slave, turns, and sees her husband.

"Richard!" She appears surprised but pleased to see him. "I didn't expect you to come tonight."

He moves forward, cups her elbow with his hand and kisses her cheek. It is the closest contact they have had since the row. He starts carefully, sticking to safe ground.

"Of course I came. I wouldn't miss your show."

Richard can feel the intensity with which her eyes scan his face, looking for signs of anger, or repentance.

"Well, what did you think?"

"Magnificent, as usual. The pyrotechnics were impressive. And I see you are carrying on the fire theme in here tonight. The smell of charred skin is bringing back memories… of Danny's induction."

"Ah yes, Danny. That must have been a special day." Alannah smiles warmly before she remembers she is still angry with him. Her face falls to a frown, freezing him out. This is not going to be easy. He realises he spoke about Danny during the argument. It was unwise to mention his name now. Damn.

She changes the subject.

"New slave?" she glances at Simon.

"Yes… well, new but not mine." It was now or never. He must bite the bullet and hope she will not scorn him in front of everyone.

"Actually, I came to apologise. For what I said the other

day. It was wrong of me. I acted unfairly, and I'm sorry."

She turns her head away and puts one hand on her hip in annoyance.

"You're doing this here? Tonight?" She shakes her head angrily. "Richard, I'm working. Do you really think this is the time and place?"

He swallows forcefully. This is more difficult than he'd hoped. Perhaps she is not yet willing to reconcile after such a major error on a sensitive topic. She is probably still angry with him, perhaps angry enough to continue the argument in public. What's worse, every Domme and slave in the room is staring at them, not even pretending to go about their business. This could be an embarrassing miscalculation. But there is no way backwards, he is committed and he must press on.

"You're right, of course. This isn't the time or place to talk. Perhaps we can go out for dinner later in the week, just the two of us? So we can discuss it properly out of earshot of the slaves?" He glances around the room, wishing he was out of earshot of everyone else too, but does not voice it. "I brought it up tonight because I want to give you a gift."

She hesitates, looking at the new slave behind him, piecing together the clues but unsure of her conclusion.

"A gift?"

She is softening, thank God. Richard steps to the side and gestures towards the slave.

"A peace offering. A slave from the auction. I thought you would appreciate a change from... How did you phrase it? 'The sycophants falling at your feet claiming to be subs but dictating every last detail of the scene they want'? You've been working so hard recently. This event always takes a lot of attention, and your client diary hasn't let up for weeks. You must be tired. I thought you might enjoy having some fun on your own terms, with someone who isn't paying for your time. I thought the hair might interest you? And there's something else too..."

Alannah sizes up the slave with increasing interest. She is weighing up his offer. At least, her eyes no longer flash with anger. She appears calm. Perhaps his plan will work after all.

"Something else? Go on."

"He's a play virgin. Well, he claims to be. Apparently, he has never done a scene in public. It seems plausible enough from the sheer panic he's been showing since I bought him. He's looking for... and I quote... 'an experienced Mistress to show him what we're all here for.'"

Richard smiles mischievously, growing in confidence that Alannah is not about to tear a strip off him in public. He cocks his head flirtatiously.

"Do you think you can manage that?"

Alannah shakes her head in mock exasperation.

"Poor thing, no wonder he looks petrified. A real lamb to the slaughter, isn't he? Oh Richard, you and your grand bloody gestures. It's a good job I love you."

Relief. She will forgive him, and all will be well.

"Does that mean you'll accept him? Because your auction rules are very specific about guaranteed play. If you don't want him, then of course I will comply with the policy... But I think I might break him."

She laughs, taking the leash from his hand.

"In that case how can I refuse? It's practically my duty to rescue him from you. As for the rest… Let's talk about it over dinner. We have a lot to work out."

"We do. I think you understand the complications. But I love you, and we will find a way to make it work. Now go and enjoy yourself. Oh, and you might want this."

He hands her a package, wrapped in black tissue paper and tied with a red bow.

"What's this?" she questions, tearing open the paper.

Inside is a hairbrush, broad and flat with a long handle. She looks up in wonder, all traces of anger gone.

"Just how long have you been planning this?"

"Ah now, woman, let me keep some of my secrets." He smiles, satisfied that the rift in their relationship is healing.

"Thank you. It's a very thoughtful gift. Will you stay to watch? Shall I have someone bring you a drink."

"No, my love, I have Sarah waiting. I better take her home, she needs to be up tomorrow to prepare for my 1 o'clock. Unless there's anything you need?"

"No, I think Mistress Stephanie and I have everything in hand. In that case I'll see you at home tomorrow. I expect I'll sleep late, so I'll see you after your clients have gone?"

"Yes. I'll have Danny cook something for dinner. Just the four of us. In the mean time… enjoy your gift and don't work too hard."

With a nod, he glances at the slave, and leaves.

Eight

The Playroom

———

Stepping over the threshold of the metal door, awareness begins to trickle into the drunken treacle of Simon's consciousness. The private playroom. Mistress Alannah.

Recognition gives way to a yearning sensation, muddled with icy trepidation. Is she the Mistress he will be given to? On stage, she was the embodiment of his fantasy. Up there she was unreachable, and he was safely hidden in the crowd. But at close quarters, she is dreadfully real.

Orange licks of flame grip his attention and send shivers down his spine, only releasing his gaze when they snake into the water and sizzle out.

Wide eyed, he observes the interaction between the Master and the Mistress. They know each other? Damn, of course they know each other. This is her event, so obviously she is well connected in the London fetish scene. And Master Richard is notorious, Kate had made that clear. They are bound to know each other. But it seems more than that. There is a subtext, something he does not understand. In fact, Master Richard seems rather uneasy. Could it be that he, too, is under her spell?

His confusion deepens as Richard steps forward and kisses her cheek. Simon's hackles rise at the idea of Mistress Alannah allowing herself to be touched by this unclean thing, by this man whose reputation is for violence and depravity. A sudden urge to protect her. And envy, too.

When the Master speaks the line from the auction catalogue, and Simon burns with shame. He bores his eyes into a spot on the floor, as rising anger thuds in his ears. They are laughing at him. This cruel bastard is making a joke of his inexperience, and she is laughing at him.

Simon's hands clench, ready to swing a punch or else to reach for the collar fastening and bolt. Before he can act, she reaches forward and takes hold of his leash. His eyes flick upwards, and with surprise he sees that her face is kind, and her green eyes are full of concern. She is not mocking him.

He returns his gaze to the floor, stomach churning, as the adrenaline weakens its grip. He barely registers the rest of their conversation, or the surreal parcel which opens to reveal a hairbrush.

Finally, the Master leaves.

Simon licks his lips and tries to swallow. He feels dull, slowed down more by the weight of his emotions than by the alcohol. He does not know what he should expect, or how to please his Mistress. Will she want to whip him, too? To cut his back open and make him scream in pain?

That is not something he wants to endure. Once again, he considers fleeing before it is too late. But the metal door is shut tight, and paradoxically inaction feels safer than the alternative. Meekly, he waits for instruction.

*

Alannah yawns and stretches her shoulders out.

Turning to Simon, the corner of her mouth lifts playfully into a half-smile.

"So, are you as terrified as you look?"

Her voice is warm and kind. Friendly, even. Not what he expected at all. He finds himself wanting her approval, wanting to please her. He struggles to find his voice to reply, shyly.

"Yes, Mistress."

Mirth glints in her eyes.

"Don't worry. We'll take things slowly. There's no reason to be afraid."

Her words sound so plausible, even comforting. And yet, how can they be true? This is Mistress Alannah, professional Dominatrix, and the woman he'd just watched torturing someone with a flaming bullwhip. Simon's fear will not be quelled.

She turns away and calls to her second in command.

"Mistress Stephanie, please would you instruct the door guards to turn away the remaining queue. I am quite worn out. I think I will make this new toy my last amusement of the evening."

Stephanie nods. "Of course, Mistress. Would you like

to look over the admission figures? Or the report from security?"

"No, thank you, they can wait until tomorrow. Please would you check whether the playroom Dommes have anything which needs my immediate attention, and everything else can be sent to me at home. In the meantime, I have some aftercare to administer." She nods at Stephanie, and looks back towards the figure tied to the St Andrew's cross. Then her eyes slide towards Simon and the half smile reappears on her lips.

"But first, let's put you somewhere out of the way until I'm ready to deal with you."

Mistress Alannah leads Simon to the side of the room, where two ornate chairs stand either side of a table. She lays the hairbrush on the table, turns to him and instructs, "Sit down."

Simon moves toward the chair, but something makes him hesitate. He glances back at Mistress Alannah's face. Her eyebrows are raised in surprise. No, not surprise. Distaste. Shit, he thinks, what have I done wrong?

She shakes her head, and repeats, "Down." She tugs at the rope, indicating with her eyes the place she expects him to sit.

The floor. Oh God, of course, he's supposed to sit on the floor, not on the chair. A stupid mistake. The simplest instruction and he can't even get that right. What must she think of him?

Nervously, he drops to the floor, half kneeling, half sitting. He starts to speak an apology, but falters, tongue tied. Instead, he hangs his head low, and blushes.

A heartbeat later, she is at his side, crouching down beside him. Right next to him. He can smell her perfume, and feel the warmth of her body almost brushing his shoulder. Almost – but not quite. Her presence is comforting and threatening all at once.

As suddenly as she was near him, she is gone. Her warmth recedes away as she stands up and takes a step away. He realises, then, what she has done. His rope leash is now tied to the leg of the chair. He is captive once more.

She looks down on him kindly.

"Stay here until I am free to see to you," she instructs. "Do you need anything before I go back to finish my work?"

He does not want her to go, not even just a few steps away. Others are engaged in scenes around the room, and he doesn't want to be left alone. But he doesn't know how to explain without sounding stupid. Most of all he doesn't want to disappoint her again. For lack of any other words to say, he answers simply.

"No, Mistress."

"Good. I will be back soon." She walks away from him, towards a medical trolley at the back of the room.

*

Alannah yawns again as she walks away from her gift, towards the stash of bandages, sprays and sterilizing wipes. Tired she may be, but Richard's present is a good one. Long hair, something she always takes pleasure from. And those puppy dog eyes, so earnest and so fearful. She rarely plays with submissives that are this innocent, especially now that her London client list is well established. Her tribute fee puts off all but the most financially solvent of committed slaves.

Oh, Richard. He owed her a huge apology, and he has made one. She is relieved he has calmed down and offered the olive branch – and a very well selected olive branch at that. His choice demonstrates how well he understands her. And the fact that he had the gall to apologise here, in public. She knows how difficult that would be, for a man like him. Despite their differences, she agrees they will find a way to make things work, and will move forward all the stronger for it. She knows her colleagues wonder why she married him, but Alannah cannot imagine loving anyone else.

And of course, it is only good manners to make sure she thoroughly enjoys her gift.

But first she must complete her duties for the night.

Picking up an antiseptic spray from the metal tray, Alannah strides back towards the X-shaped cross which holds the damaged remains of her previous slave.

Nine

A Beginning

Simon waits quietly as Mistress Alannah unties her victim and begins to treat his wounds. He tries not to watch. It makes him nervous about what might be in store for him.

He lets his eyes wander across the room to another pair who are engaged in a scene to his left, a few meters from where he kneels. Mistress Stephanie sits on a high stool, one foot resting on the chest of a man who lies supine beneath her. She wears knee high leather boots with curved metal heels. Her legs are crossed, her higher foot dangling close to the man's face. He is licking one boot whilst she pushes the heel of the other into his ribs. Not just licking, but slathering his whole mouth across the sole, licking round the pointed toe, then back down to the sole again to suck at the heel. The man's enjoyment is obvious as much from his enthusiasm as from the bulge at his crotch. Simon feels squeamish watching him doing something so disgusting. The man slows down, but Mistress Stephanie encourages him along with little kicks down his stomach. Not satisfied, she grinds the toe of her boot into the man's groin. Simon flinches, repulsed, and closes his eyes in a grimace.

"You get used to it."

Mistress Alannah's voice, behind him, makes him jump. She has finished with her slave and come for him.

"Other people's preferences, I mean. You get used to seeing people do things you don't enjoy yourself. It's all about consent. Once you trust that your limits will be respected, you stop worrying about being forced to do things that turn you off. When your fear is gone, it's easier to watch others draw pleasure from their kinks, whilst you draw pleasure from yours."

It makes sense, in a twisted sort of way. Simon nods.

"Yes, Mistress."

She walks around the chair, and stands in front of him. His face is level with her thighs, which flow up out of her boots, disappearing under her too-short skirt. The flamed corset encircles her hips, sweeping upwards to a tightly laced waist.

"So now, we need to talk about your limits, and negotiate what I am going to do with you."

His dick twitches, but his racing mind wins out. This is not a fantasy, this is real. He is actually here, in the private playroom of a Dominatrix. She has just cut a man's back open with a whip, and she's expecting to do God knows what to him. Fuck, this was a stupid idea. What the hell is he doing here? He shakes his head and tries to stand up.

"I'm sorry, this is a mistake. I can't do this. I need to go."

Swiftly she places one hand on his shoulder, gently pressing him downwards. She kneels, bringing her face to the same level as his, as if he were a child. For a minute she simply looks at him, watching his expression. Simon feels his resolve weaken. He stills, then sinks back to the floor.

"You really are terrified, aren't you?" she asks, not unkindly. "You can leave if you want to. Right now, or any time in the future. No one will stop you. But I mean what I said. Nothing will happen without your consent. There is no reason to be afraid. We will take things slowly."

She pauses to let her words sink in.

"Do you want me to release you right now?"

Simon looks into her perfect green eyes, circled in black with flawless makeup. Her long lashes blink as she waits for his answer. She is serene, a calming presence. He feels his perspective twist, and his fear begins to dissipate. The words fall out before he realises he is defeated.

"No, Mistress."

Her eyes soften with pleasure.

"Good. Thank you for trusting me. We are going to talk. Just talk. That is how we shall begin. Is that OK?"

"Yes, Mistress."

*

Alannah stands, walks to the corner and returns pushing a tall wheeled mirror. She aligns it a few paces from the slave, then sinks into the chair beside him. They both face the mirror. She crosses her legs, laying one long laced boot over the other. In the reflection, she surveys the virgin plaything on the floor beside her. Richard was right, he is nervous. Nervous, but eager. She will proceed cautiously. This is going to be fun. It's just a shame she is so tired.

Thank God she kept the mirror. It takes up a lot of space, she was thinking of getting rid of it, but she is glad of it tonight. It will be much better to see his face while she plays. Better, and necessary with a new slave. She needs to watch his reaction and gauge how he is coping. Not that her plans for him involve much to cope with… not yet, at least. Perhaps later. But only if he doesn't run away before they get going properly. Without laying a finger on him, she begins.

"So, let's start with something straightforward. Tell me your name."

"Simon, Mistress."

"Good." She smiles. "And is this your first time at one of my parties, Simon?"

"Yes, Mistress."

"Have you attended any other fetish events?"

"Only one other, Mistress. A small club in South London. It was nothing like tonight. I'm pretty new to all of this."

She watches as he drops his eyes to the floor, blushing. She smiles, amused.

"Well, my ball isn't aimed as an entry level event Simon. Most of our guests have been in the scene for years. But you appear to be a little different from the norm. Is it true, then, what Richard said? That you've never played a scene in public before?"

His cheeks flush hotter. His shame is fascinating. He must be very new.

"Yes, Mistress, it's true. To be honest, I'm not really sure what I'm doing here. I had this idea about what it would be like. But the reality is a bit more… well, it's just… it's different than I imagined."

"I hope we haven't disappointed you?"

"Oh no, Mistress. It's the opposite really. It's hard to explain."

"Please try. I'd like to be certain what you mean."

"I thought it would be more like a role play I guess – like a fantasy. I didn't expect it to be so… so real."

So it is true. He is completely new. Unschooled and unblemished. A clean slate to leave her imprint on, like walking on fresh snow.

She has to admit, Richard has outdone himself. A virgin slave, with flowing golden locks. The boy is a superb choice, exactly what she needs to forget the demands of her client list. A slave worth an unhurried beginning. If he can be persuaded, of course. The first step is reassurance.

"That's OK. I understand. There's no need to be embarrassed. Everyone must start at the beginning, and new things feel uncertain. We all learn as we go along, even the most committed of sexual deviants is on a journey. But coming here… well, you did rather jump off the deep end. How on earth did you end up in my slave auction?"

This is one answer Simon is sure of.

"Kate."

"Kate? Your girlfriend?"

"No, Mistress. We're just friends. Actually I met her at work."

Alannah nods but stays silent, and Simon finds himself recounting the entire story.

"I'd just split up with my girlfriend. The whole team went out to celebrate the project release. I got a bit drunk, and ended up crying on Kate's shoulder. I should have kept my mouth shut, but I told her everything. About… you know. What my girlfriend liked to do to me. When she ended it, I thought I'd never find someone else who liked that too. But subconsciously I must have known Kate was a safe person to tell. It turns out she likes being submissive too. She told me about the fetish scene, and sort of persuaded me to try it. It's really hard to say no to her. So we came here. She wanted to find a Dom, so she decided to sign up for the slave auction, and she just kind of dragged me along too."

Alannah giggles. So naïve.

"My goodness, bullied into the auction by a submissive? You really do need some training." She smiles reassuringly. "I think you and I are going to have a lot of fun together, Simon. I do like a man who can't say no." Her tone is playful, but her eyes let slip the hint of a threat which sends a tingle down Simon's spine. How can he fear this, yet want it so badly?

"And I think it's time we took things a step further, don't you?"

Simon's spine jolts again. He doesn't know what answer to give. What is she planning? He frowns, uncertain.

"Please Mistress… I don't want to be whipped. Not like the last guy."

She shakes her head.

"I wouldn't dream of it."

His lips part and his eyebrows furrow.

"You wouldn't?"

"Of course not. That was a heavy scene. It might leave scars. Do you think I would do such a thing without careful planning?"

He still looks unsure.

"I have known that particular volunteer for several months. We discussed the idea twice before tonight. I will only do something like that if I am certain the slave truly desires the scene and understand the risks."

"Oh." He sounds a little deflated.

"That's not the sort of thing I have in mind for you at all."

He shudders. Alannah pushes on, giving him no time to panic.

"I'm going to tell you a secret. It's an open secret, really, but one that is often forgotten by my… professional friends. You see, I have a few fetishes of my own." She hesitates, to draw his interest. The tactic works, and he looks up at her reflection, intrigued.

"I have a preference for long hair." She leans forward, whispering into his ear conspiratorially. "I always have. I can't really explain why, that's what makes it a fetish. I simply enjoy it. Long, straight hair. The feeling of it, the way it moves, the sensation of it sliding over my skin." Gazing into the mirror, her pupils dilate, round and black and inviting. "Richard knows this about me. Now do you understand why he chose you? Why he bought you for me, and gave me this hairbrush?"

"I… I think so Mistress."

"Simon…" another pause, a lascivious parting of her lips. "Simon, I like your hair. I want to brush it. And whilst I am brushing it, you are going to sit very still and be very good, and we will talk. Does that sound like something you would like?"

Bemused, Simon nods. It seems implausible that such a simple thing would please her, but he wouldn't dare to say so. Besides, the idea that something about his body might arouse her… God, it makes the fantasies in his head start to bleed into reality again.

"Then come and sit closer, near my feet. Face the mirror. Make sure you are comfortable, I don't want you moving around."

"Yes, Mistress."

He scoots himself sideways, watching her as she uncrosses her legs, placing one knee either side of his shoulders. As she moves, her leg brushes his back. Flesh on flesh, a sudden intimacy.

"Now, take off your top."

Simon stalls, uncomfortable at the idea of being half naked despite the flimsiness of his shirt. Mistress Alannah's displeasure is clear, in sharp contrast to her previous friendly disposition.

"I expect you to obey my commands. Quickly, and without question. Take off your top. Now."

All gentleness has drained from her tone, rousing

trepidation in the pit of Simon's stomach. This emotional roller coaster is too new to him. He cannot predict the changes of pace, backwards and forwards between fear and desire, pleasing her and disappointing her.

Shamed, and keen to avoid further reprimand, he obeys. Quickly he slides the mesh up and over his head, then lets it go, leaving it hanging on the rope leash between his collar and the chair. He crosses his legs and straightens his body, sitting upright in front of her.

The kindness returns to her voice.

"That's better."

*

Simon closes his eyes and sits still as stone as Mistress Alannah leans over him, like a cat guarding its kill. Gently, she lays her hands on his temples, palms smoothing down the golden hair, past his ears and towards the back, gathering the strands as she goes. It is heavy, silken. Just the right thickness – not coarse like some blondes, and not so fine that it is without weight. Good.

She slides her hands around the full volume of it, bringing them together at the ponytail. Annoyingly, the back of his head is damp with sweat and underneath the hair sticks to his skin. It will dry, but the imperfection irritates her. The hair will not be at its best until it is washed, which isn't an option here. Such a shame.

Slowly, she begins to pull at the hair tie, sliding it down the length to remove it. It slips one, then two inches before getting stuck. Feeling gently underneath, she finds that the buckle of the auction collar has snared up in the soft hairs there.

Carefully, she begins to untangle the knots from the buckle. She succeeds in gently releasing most of the hair, but a small strand will not come away. It remains firmly wedged in the metal, somehow caught in a gap in the buckle prong. It will not yield. She frowns. This is not how she wants this to be. Damn cheap collars. No, she will not waste time coaxing the tangle out. It will have to be the quick way.

She takes hold of the strand between her thumb and forefinger, braces her other hand on the buckle, and rips it free.

Sudden pain forces Simon to take a sharp breath. His eyes open wide in surprise. His shoulders stiffen, but he does not pull away from her touch. Holding absolutely still, she watches him in the mirror while his breath returns to normal and his shoulders relax down. Those puppy dog eyes seem to be more upset that she hurt him than by the pain itself. Delicious. Alannah purrs at his discomfort.

"Yes, I think you and I could have a lot of fun together." Her voice is deep and honey sweet, like a lover's.

Simon smiles shyly. He does not welcome the pain. But God, the look of her when it happened. All hunger and possessiveness. And that sound she made. Knowing that he caused it, even passively, stirs arousal. He would do anything to please her more. To let her use his body for her enjoyment.

*

Resuming, Alannah twists the collar, sliding it around the slave's neck so the buckle lies out of the way on one side, and rope leash runs from the other. She eases the tie down the full length of his hair and releases it. Picking up the hairbrush, she begins.

Starting at the ends, and gradually, ever so gradually, working her way upwards to the roots, she ekes out the knots from each part. Brushing over and over again, she lets the hair fall over her wrists and slide between her fingers. She allows her full attention to be absorbed in the blonde waterfall. With a lilting rhythm of hand then brush, hand then brush, she runs each from temple to shoulder as if stroking a pet.

Eyes closed once more, Simon sits at her feet, letting her soothe away his fear. Tingles dance over his scalp and slide down his spine. His breathing is jagged and shallow. God, she has barely touched him and already he is so turned on simply by the way she looks at him. He is little more than an impotent toy under her control. But she wants him, and he pleases her, and that is everything. All the old fantasies and imagined situations hinge on this. That Mistress chooses me to be her plaything. That I can rouse her desire and be its satisfaction. Sighing, he submits under the movement of her hands.

Ten

Negotiation

———

Alannah indulges in a few blissful moments smoothing and brushing her new pet before picking up the conversation.

"So, slave. How are you doing?"

"Fine, Mistress, thank you."

A yawn escapes her lips. She rolls her head to loosen her neck.

"Good boy. Now, tell me about this girlfriend. The one who introduced you to submission."

The slave shifts uncomfortably, but she lets it pass without comment.

"At first it was just a normal relationship. We went out on a few dates, hung out at each other's places, that sort of thing."

"And then…?"

Simon swallows, reaching for the right words.

"Well… erm…"

"I won't judge you. I simply want to know what you're used to, so I can work out what we might enjoy doing together. Otherwise how will I know where to start our negotiation?"

"Negotiation, Mistress?" He looks confused.

"You don't think I'll be satisfied simply by brushing your hair, do you?"

"No, Mistress." He blushes again, a small smile plays on his lips.

"Well?"

He hesitates. "Well, it was when we were in bed."

"Go on."

"She liked to tie me up. To the bed. And she blindfolded me, so she could do whatever she liked to me."

"And what, exactly, did she like to do?"

Mistress Alannah's hands continued to soothe their sensuous rhythm through his hair. Simon is sure she can sense the growing throbbing in his groin.

"Mostly she liked to sit on my face, Mistress."

Alannah laughs.

"Sure, so restraint, blindfolding and queening. What else?"

"Well, she would have sex with me too, Mistress."

"OK. Anything else? So far there's not much to work with that isn't directly sexual."

"I don't understand, Mistress?"

Alannah's eyebrows arch, and her hands stop moving.

"I do hope you're not expecting to get laid in my playroom, Simon."

"Oh... no, Mistress. I didn't mean... I wouldn't presume... Of course not, Mistress."

His flushed face betrays his lie. She shakes her head in frustration. Suddenly his eagerness seems much less appealing. Perhaps he is too naïve. Not that there is anything inherently wrong with sex as part of play. But to hope for it so soon... and with her... she shudders.

"This is not the Pen at Club Pain. If you want to get fucked you should have stayed with Master Richard."

Simon looks horrified.

"Oh no, Mistress. I don't like men. Not like that. I'm straight. And I didn't mean... I'm sorry." He trails off and falls quiet.

Still, at least he knows enough to backpedal. And his hair is beautiful. And it can be amusing to crawl inside the mind of a fresh one, to toy with him for a while before making him come so hard he loses the ability to speak. Once, she had one who lost his mind so completely that, afterwards, he did nothing but whimper for two hours. This one seems the type to set a new record. If she was in that sort of a mood.

But not here, not at the ball. It would have to be somewhere else. Somewhere a little more private.

Absentmindedly, she strokes a lock with the back of her forefinger, and decides to give him the benefit of the doubt.

"Let's try this another way. When you signed up for the slave auction, what did you hope might happen?"

"I thought that whoever bought me would take me to the playroom, Mistress."

"And?"

"And maybe we would try out some of the equipment. I've only ever been tied up in bed. I thought it might be interesting to try being tied upright on a frame, or face down over a bench."

"Good. That's a start at least. Was there any particular kind of restraint you had in mind? Leather cuffs? Metal chains? Rope?"

"I don't know Mistress. It was handcuffs before. I'd like to try something different."

"I don't like using metal cuffs. Dreadful things. Fine for role play games, but bad as restraints. The wrists are very delicate, and weight bearing on metal edges can do serious damage. Have you tried leather ones?"

"No, Mistress."

"It's hard to go wrong with a nice wide leather cuff. Something padded, with locking posts and at least two D rings. They can be tied with ropes, chains, or even straps, in any number of imaginative positions."

"I think I'd like that, Mistress."

"Very well. And what did you imagine might happen after you are tied?"

"Well… Kate says I should try something called a violet wand, Mistress."

"They can be fun, yes. Do you have any medical conditions? Any heart problems?"

"No, Mistress."

"Good, then there is no reason we couldn't play with a wand. Does Kate have any more suggestions?"

"She keeps telling me about riding crops, but I'm not

sure I'm interested in pain, Mistress."

"Oh, the crop doesn't have to be painful, unless you want it to be. There are ways to build up the intensity slowly so the burning sensation is more prominent than the pain. Quick and shallow, that's the trick. I bet I could work up a nice red glow on your backside, Simon, and I bet you'd like it so much your cock gets all red and hard too."

Simon shivers at the unexpected directness of her words. He can't think of anything to say. He can feel his face burning, and that only makes him think about what she just said all the more.

Alannah laughs.

"Poor thing. Forgive me, I'm just teasing you. To see how you react. It's rather sweet when you blush like that."

Her compliment does nothing to reduce the heat in his cheeks.

*

Mistress Alannah falls quiet for a few moments, allowing the focus to return to the reassuring rhythm of her hands. Best to introduce it indirectly, so the idea slides into the conversation, almost naturally. The wand is the key, that's the lever to manoeuvre him with.

"So, tell me a little more about yourself, Simon. Do you live in London, or did you travel to come here?"

"I live here, Mistress. Zone 3, but still on the night buses." Good, so there is no hotel room waiting for him.

"And who do you live with? Is it this Kate, who I

keep hearing about?" It had better not be with his family. Nothing is more of a turn off than the thought of an anxious mother waiting for the safe return of her wayward offspring.

"No, Mistress, not Kate. It's just a flat share, Mistress. There are four of us. Most of us know each other from Uni, but every couple of months someone moves out and someone else moves in."

Flatmates. A bachelor pad, from the sounds of it. If they go out on a Saturday night, it's likely sometimes one of them to fails to come home. Good. That will suit her plan well.

"And do you have any exciting plans for the rest of the weekend?"

A hint of confusion on his face, perhaps he is piecing things together already?

"Not really, Mistress. We'll just crash out on the sofa and watch a couple of films, maybe order pizza. Usually someone has a killer hangover on Sunday, so we keep it pretty relaxed."

"That's good. Because you and I have a problem, Simon."

"A problem, Mistress?"

He is drifting blindly into her trap, still thinking they are having a cosy chat. He is very naïve. And very much in her thrall, from the shy breathy way he answers her questions. It should be easy enough to overcome his fears and persuade him.

"Yes. Two problems, in fact."

"I'm sorry, Mistress. I don't understand."

"Well, I am far too tired to enjoy you properly tonight. And... I don't have any violet wands here."

"You don't? Well, it was just an idea, Mistress. We could do something else, if you want?"

She smiles, leaving a pause that is just a little uncomfortably long. Her hands continue to smooth through his hair. It really will be better after it's washed. Perhaps some oil, too.

"No, I think it's a very good suggestion for a first scene. But..."

She stops, changing tack before closing in to finish it.

"Simon, have you ever done something which you knew was a bad idea?"

His eyes flick down and to the left. He is wrestling with the idea. Trying to guess what she means.

"Like what, Mistress?"

"I mean, something which feels exciting, but also seems risky?"

"Like signing up for your slave auction, Mistress?"

She laughs, and he smiles back, confused but still trusting.

"A little like that, I suppose. You see, I would like to strap you to a bench and do all those things we've talked about." She pauses again, eyeing up various parts of his body until the glow in his cheeks returns. "But Simon... all of my violet wands are at home."

"Oh. OK, well..." She cuts him off.

"I wonder if you can be persuaded to come home with me? You can sleep at the house tonight, and in the morning I can take my time with you. My promise still stands, you can leave at any point you want. I'll make sure you get home safely afterwards."

She can almost hear his inner voice telling him it's unwise to go alone to any stranger's house, especially in these circumstances. Deliberately, she interrupts his train of thought by stroking her fingertips behind his ear, and softly down the side of his neck. Suggestion and control.

"I want to be absolutely clear. I'm not going to fuck you, Simon. This is not some one night stand. What I'm offering you is something quite different. First, sleep. And tomorrow, an unhurried scene with time to explore both our interests. At the risk of boasting, when I offer that kind of one to one attention it usually comes with a lot of zeros on the price tag. But I don't have any plans tomorrow, and I like you. I want to break you in gently. Come home with me, Simon. I promise you won't regret it."

He shivers again, then ever so slightly tilts his head toward her touch. There. She has him. When he speaks, his words only confirm what she already knows.

"Yes, Mistress. I'll come. If you want me to."

Eleven

Home

Fifteen minutes later, Simon follows behind Mistress Alannah, down a backstage corridor towards the rear door. He carries his coat, rucksack, and Mistress' jacket over his arm. His cloakroom ticket had been surrendered to a uniformed guard who fetched his belongings. Another guard had been sent to summon the car. Simon himself had not left Mistress' side.

Click click click. The noise of her heels resonates on the concrete floor. The echo emphasises that they are alone together. His leash is short, and he has to concentrate to avoid tangling his feet with hers, tripping them both. She appears unconcerned, or unaware of the danger.

The corridor ends in a fire door. As they reach it, she stops and gestures at her jacket, waiting until Simon takes the hint and holds it out for her to slip over her shoulders. She smiles reassuringly, and pushes open the door.

Outside, the air is cold and slightly damp. A large black Bentley is waiting. She hesitates momentarily, then strides into the alley towards the car.

A man steps out of the driver's seat; a man wearing large black sunglasses, and a white satin jumpsuit embellished with rhinestones. He has an unconvincing quaffed wig on his head. Elvis, or a cheap version of him, is to be their driver. It would feel surreal, but Simon has already fallen too far down the rabbit hole to have any surprise left.

"Good evening Ma'am. Where can I take you?"

"Good evening, Elvis. Straight home, please."

"Sure thing, Ma'am." He opens the rear door, and nods a greeting at Simon, who climbs inside and scoots across the leather seat to the far side of the car. The inside is large, with seats facing front and back. A steel ring on a tether plate is bolted in the middle of the floor. Mistress Alannah slips into the place next to him. Elvis shuts the door, and returns to the driver's seat.

"You got back quickly, Elvis. I thought we might have to wait."

"The roads are pretty clear this time of night, Ma'am. And my mama taught me never to keep a lady waiting if I could help it, Ma'am."

She hums her approval before taking out her phone to check her messages.

The car glides through the wet streets, heading north east, past old brick warehouses and glass offices. At first the streets are familiar, then they grow strange. Occasionally they pass a tube station, allowing Simon a sense of the direction in which they are heading. Mistress Alannah is occupied typing into her phone. She neither speaks to him nor pays him any heed at all. The driver steals glances in the rear view mirror but doesn't say a word. Simon concentrates on the scenes speeding past his window, trying not to think about what might happen when they arrive at their destination.

After twenty minutes or so, the car pulls over and stops outside a Victorian house, set back from the main road. A low lying wall separates the front garden from the pavement. Overgrown hedges and a few tall trees shield the face of the house from clear view. One flank, more visible from the car has chimney breasts snaking up the outside, revealing that the house was once part of a terrace before it was bombed out in the War. Now it sits alone, incongruous, between a retail park and an office block.

Elvis gets out of the car, and opens the door for Mistress Alannah. She pivots her boots out of the door, and gracefully rises up from the car. Simon feels a pressure at his throat and realises she is still holding his rope leash. Quickly, he grabs his rucksack and scrambles across to get out of the car. Elvis shuts the door behind him.

"Is there anything else you'll be needing now, Ma'am?"

"That will be all tonight, thank you Elvis. I will call you tomorrow to take this slave away. It won't be early."

"Whatever you say, Ma'am. I hope you have a pleasant night, Ma'am." He half-nods half-bows at Mistress Alannah, then smirks at Simon. "Sir." Simon has no chance to respond before he turns to shut the door and drops back behind the wheel. A bus judders past, radiating fluorescent light across the street. Faces stare out, then are gone.

Alannah fishes in her jacket pocket for her key, and takes a step towards the tiled path.

"Welcome to my home, Simon."

✻

The old black and white diamonds are covered in leaves, treacherously slippery in the rain. Simon wonders how Mistress keeps her footing in those boots. A few meters past the hedge, a stone staircase rises five steps towards a broad door under a semi-circular fanlight. A brief rattle of the key in the lock and the door swings open, admitting them to a long hallway with wooden floors. Two doors lead off to the left, and an elegant staircase curls upwards at the far end. Mistress removes her jacket and hangs it on the overloaded coat hooks by the stairs.

"You can leave your coat here. Keep your bag with you for now." Simon nods, and does as suggested.

She drapes the rope leash over the bannister, and instructs, "Stay here for one moment."

Alannah walks past the staircase towards a more modern extension at the back of the house. But before reaching it she stops, turns to face the side of the staircase, and puts one finger against her lips, mouthing "shhh" to Simon. She pushes on the wooden panels and clicks open a hidden door to a lower staircase which leads down to the basement. She disappears down the steps, returning moments later with a shackle, chain and padlocks. She smiles as if this is the most normal thing in the world, then clicks the door back into place. Simon presses his lips together and tries to focus on anything but his stiffening dick. Smiling, she picks up the rope and climbs the stairs.

Two floors up, the staircase ends. Three doors lead off the broad landing. Mistress Alannah stops.

"You don't seem very tired, Simon."

"I'm not really, Mistress. I'm a bit wired to be honest."

"That's a shame, Simon. I'm exhausted. I'm not going to play with you tonight, you understand that don't you?"

"Yes Mistress." He shifts uncomfortably, trying to hide his erection behind his rucksack.

"Good. It's time to sleep now, Simon. This is my bedroom. I expect you to behave impeccably. If you give me any trouble at all, you will regret it. Do you understand?"

"Yes, Mistress."

She leads him into one of the rooms. Inside is a dressing table, an armchair, and a large wrought iron bed. An open door leads to a bathroom, another to a dressing room lined with rails of clothes. Alannah perches on the bed, dropping the chains beside her, then pulls on Simon's rope until his face is uncomfortably close to hers.

"Would you be a sweetheart and take off my boots?"

When Simon nods, she reaches forward and slides a long finger into the D ring at his throat, removing the rope from his collar. Her lips are inches from his, full and painted bright red. He considers trying to kiss her, but thinks better of it. Instead, he drops to the floor and begins to untangle the laces. Tugging each spiked heel in turn, he slides her boots from her feet. He stands up again, uncertain what to do next.

She lazily flexes one ankle and sighs. "Good boy. And

now, my corset, please." Before he can speak, she turns around and leans over the bed, planting her palms on the mattress and pushing her body backwards. Her short skirt sticks out over her ass, which almost grazes his crotch. Simon's heartbeat pounds into every corner of his body, but he remembers her warning and realises that, despite her provocation, it would not be wise to act. He resists the urge to rub his dick against her buttocks. Instead, he concentrates on keeping his hands steady as he picks at the knot of cords behind her waist, teasing them free and gently releasing the pressure between the two halves of the stiff garment.

When it is loose, she does not unclip the fastenings but instead turns back to face him, sitting back onto the bed.

"Good boy. Now, take off your clothes."

Simon takes a moment to consider her instruction. Maybe he has been too cautious after all? He has started to undress her, and now she wants him to strip? Perhaps he might be allowed to kiss her? Perhaps she might put her hands on his body and give him some relief from this throbbing? Or is she just teasing him? Either way, it is sweet suffering.

He pulls the mesh shirt over his head, unzips his trousers and peels them off his legs. Trying not to fall over, he plucks off both socks. He stands up again before going any further. His hard on is very obvious through his shorts. Part of him is embarrassed, and part of him is unashamed. Still, he can't quite bring himself to take off his underwear. Does she actually want him naked?

Mistress Alannah smiles, amused.

"Don't stop there, Simon. You haven't taken off your collar yet."

Damn, he had forgotten the collar. Cringing, Simon unbuckles the leather and drops it to the floor.

"And…? Don't make me ask twice, Simon."

Closing his eyes, he takes a deep breath and slides off his shorts too. His dick protrudes painfully into the air in front of his stomach.

"Good boy. See, all red and hard and we didn't even need a crop."

Is she pleased? Is she threatening him? He can't tell. His face flushes almost as red as his cock.

"Come on then. Bed time."

He looks up at her, unsure what he is supposed to do. Should he get on the bed next to her? He takes a tentative step towards her.

She shakes her head. "No. Really, Simon. I made that very clear. Go to the bathroom, you will find spare toothbrushes under the sink. Take a glass of water if you want one. Then come back and get into bed. Alone."

Disappointed, he shuffles to the bathroom and closes the door. He's too hard to be able to piss easily. He waits until he softens enough, but still ends up leaning over the toilet bowl at a strange angle before he can manage it. Brushing his teeth is straightforward, at least. He splashes lukewarm water over his face, then returns to the bedroom.

In his absence, Mistress Alannah has padlocked one end of the chain to the iron frame of the bed, and the other end to the shackle. She is still wearing her loosened corset and has not undressed further. Suddenly Simon feels emotional, on the verge of tears. Choking back the sensation, he focuses on her promise that they will play a scene in the morning. It's not that she doesn't like him. She brought him into her house, didn't she? Into her bed? He just has to wait.

She throws back one corner of the duvet, and pats the bed.

"Get in, Simon. Time to sleep."

He lays down in the unfamiliar bed, feeling less self-conscious as she lays the covers over his body.

"Good boy." She walks to the bottom of the bed, peels back the sheets, and fastens the shackle on his right ankle. The padlock clicks firmly in place. She replaces the bedding, tucking it around his legs.

"Go to sleep now Simon. I'll be back in the morning. You'll be quite safe here."

"You're… you're not sleeping here, Mistress?"

She laughs instead of replying, walking to the dressing table and placing the padlock key on its surface, out of Simon's reach.

"Goodnight, Simon. Sleep well." She walks to the door and switches off the light. "Oh, and Simon…"

"Yes, Mistress?"

"No masturbating. And absolutely no orgasms without my permission. Do you understand?"

Her words make his frustrated dick throb even more.

"Yes, Mistress."

She walks out of the room. Simon hears her descending the stairs.

He lies in the dark for a long time, kept awake by anticipation and unfulfilled desires, listening to the unfamiliar sounds of the old house as it creaks and cools in the night. Full of worry and hope, he struggles to drift off. Eventually, several hours later, he falls asleep.

Twelve

Awakening

Simon wakes slowly from a deep sleep. Some kind of noise disturbed him – but it has stopped now. He can't remember what it was. It is very warm under the duvet, and he is fuzzy headed. The sunlight streaming in under the curtains is bright – it must be late morning already. He shifts his position, feeling the heavy weight around his ankle with sharp exhilaration. He thinks back to the previous night, not quite believing he has done something this crazy. But it is true. Here he is, in the home of Mistress Alannah, lying naked in her bed God knows where in North East London. He wonders why he doesn't feel afraid? He isn't, despite the circumstances. The only sensation he feels is anticipation.

The noise starts again. It is a low buzzing, coming from somewhere in the corner of the room. In his sleepy haze, Simon does not recognise it immediately. Then, his mind brings it into focus. A phone. His mobile, ringing on silent, inside his rucksack.

Force of habit makes him throw back the covers and slide across the bed towards his bag. He manages to get one leg on the floor before the other reaches the limit of the chain, restraining his ankle behind him on top of the bed. Leaning at full stretch, he still cannot reach the bag. He looks around but there is nothing to use as a lasso. Defeated, he gives up. The buzzing ceases, as if the phone understands he is unable to help it.

He climbs awkwardly back onto the bed. It is more difficult than sliding off, since one of his legs is held at a strange high angle behind him. He is fully awake now. He notices with horror that his clothes are gone from the place he discarded them, on the floor next to the bed. Someone has been in the room whilst he slept. Perhaps Mistress, or perhaps someone else. Simon finds the thought unnerving. How long has he been asleep? Where is she?

With no alternative, he lies back down on the bed and covers himself with the duvet. It is still warm, but he can't get comfortable. He wonders who was trying to call him. How long will he have to wait for Mistress to appear?

As if summoned by his thoughts, the door opens and Alannah enters the room. She is wearing a printed green and black robe, the silk so sheer it leaves nothing to the imagination. Her hair is loose and she is barefoot.

"Good morning, Simon."

"Good morning, Mistress." The words feel strange in the light of the morning. A parody of the fantasy from the night before, when the drink and the darkness gave it credibility.

"I thought I heard you moving around. Have you been awake long?"

"No Mistress. I just woke up. Sorry, I was trying to reach my phone, someone called me."

"Hmmm. I should have confiscated that last night. I was too tired to think of it. Never mind. I'm feeling much better this morning. Are you still happy with our plan for today?"

His heart flips. Self-consciously, he replies "Erm... yes, Mistress. I'm a bit nervous, I guess. But I'd still like to... to serve you Mistress."

She smiles. "Good boy. That's exactly what I hoped you'd say. Don't worry, I won't be too cruel. I'm going to break you in ever so gently. But, first things first. Are you hungry?"

Food. Under the circumstances, Simon had forgotten all about eating. Now he thinks about it, he is hungry. His stomach adds its opinion by rumbling. "Yes, Mistress. Starving."

"I thought we could have croissants for breakfast. With tea, unless you're one of those awful coffee drinkers? Nothing too heavy on your stomach, or it won't settle well before playtime."

Playtime. Oh God, that thought sends the blood rushing into his dick. He shifts position under the duvet, but accidentally clanks the chain against the bed frame. Shit. Concentrate, Simon. Focus on the question.

"Thank you Mistress, that sounds good. Tea is fine."

She slides a phone from her pocket, and makes a call.

"Danny, are you busy right now? ... Good. Did you

go to the bakery this morning? … How many croissants are left? … Be a sweetheart and bring up them up to my bedroom, would you? With tea and some of your jam? … Yes, for two please. As quickly as you can."

Danny. Who the hell is Danny? One of Mistress' slaves? Does he live here? Simon recalls his missing clothes. Was that Danny's doing, or hers? Or is there some other explanation?

She hangs up, and smiles cheerfully at him.

"Now, Simon, how are we going to pass the time whilst we are waiting for our breakfast?"

She sits on the bed next to him, one leg folded beneath her, the other dangling down to the floor. As she does, the silk of her dressing gown falls open, slipping off her knee and revealing the inside of her thigh. It falls further, revealing more; almost too much, but still not quite indecent…

Simon realises he is staring and quickly closes his mouth and averts his gaze. Not soon enough.

"Oh dear, Simon. I was going to unchain you, but I'm not sure you can be trusted just yet."

Hot blood fills his cheeks, and pounds through his dick in unison. The humiliation somehow turns him on even more.

"Sorry, Mistress. I didn't mean to look… I wouldn't… I mean I know you don't want to… Oh God. I'm sorry, Mistress. I'm not used to this. I'm not sure what's allowed and what isn't. I don't want to do anything wrong."

She laughs. "Oh, poor boy. That's exactly why you need training. I will help you. Let's keep things simple to start with. You can look, but you must never touch. Never. Unless I give my permission first. Do you understand?"

"Yes, Mistress."

"You will not touch me, or my toys, or my equipment, or even your own body, unless I tell you to. Understand?"

"Yes, Mistress."

"Good. On the other hand, I can touch you. Anywhere and anyhow I please. If you don't like what I am doing, you can use the safe word 'Stop'. I will go slowly, so you have enough time to object before we work up to anything you dislike or find too painful. Those will be our rules for today. Do you understand?"

So she is going to touch him. Simon's balls are aching, and the throbbing in his dick intensifies. He can only nod in response.

"Can I trust you to obey those rules at all times, Simon? Because it's important that I can trust you. Otherwise we are not going to have much fun." She stands up, and begins unknotting the belt of her robe.

Oh God. Oh shit. She is taking off her robe. Oh God, what is she going to do? Somehow, he manages to whisper, "Yes, Mistress."

She unties the belt and drops each end beside her. Only her arms, wrapped across her waist, hold the silk in place.

"Because, if you lay one finger on me, Simon, without my express permission, you will very quickly be handed over to someone who will relish the chance to touch you without your permission. Someone who will take great pleasure in returning the favour tenfold. Do you understand me, Simon?"

It is a clear threat, but Simon is more interested in what she is doing with her robe. She is running one hand up the edge of the silk. She starts to lift it away from her chest, widening the V-shape of skin already showing, edging the fabric towards her shoulder and letting it slide lower over her breasts. Simon's eyes are glued to the border between pale flesh and dark silk as it glides over her curves. Soon, surely soon it will slide over her nipple and drop to the floor...

"Do you understand me, Simon?" Her voice is stricter this time. Her hands stop; the silk balanced precariously over the curve of her breast.

Simon nods, slack jawed. She waits until he gives the proper response.

"Yes, Mistress."

She giggles, turning away and re-tying her robe.

"Oh dear, Simon! Are you still hoping I will take my clothes off and get into bed with you? Poor thing. Your understanding of submission is very strongly entangled with sexual acts, isn't it? You will have to learn to separate the two. Just because you are being topped, doesn't mean you are getting fucked."

Humiliated and hurt, Simon reacts defensively.

"You already said you don't want to fuck me. I get it, OK? We both know that I want you, and you don't want me. So I don't get why you're walking around wearing next to nothing, pretending to take your clothes off just to wind me up. What do you want from me?"

She sighs, and puts one hand on her hip.

"I like to tease, Simon. It's a game. I enjoy making

someone want what they can't have. To watch the need for it grow until it is the only thing they can think about. To reduce a grown man to begging for just the tiniest taste of pleasure."

"Well that doesn't sound like fun to me. You said you weren't going to be cruel."

"It only sounds cruel because you haven't been trained yet. No-one has shown you how immensely pleasurable it can be to linger in denial. How it intensifies the enjoyment. How, after a while, the denial itself becomes sweeter than the satisfaction. I'm going to set you on a journey to learn a better sort of pleasure, Simon. And, because you are new, and because I'm going to break you in ever so gently, if you are a very good boy for the whole of our time together then I might allow you to orgasm. But not right now. Later. How does that sound?"

Simon is somewhere between loving her and hating her, or hating that he loves her, but either way he knows he wants her to relieve his frustration by wrapping her hand around his dick. He can wait, though. He is not going to beg. He is not going to let her get under his skin like that. Except, of course, that it's already too late and who the hell is he kidding. She knows exactly what she's doing, and she can see right through him. There is little point in hiding what he wants.

"That sounds good, Mistress… Thank you." The words stick in his throat, feeling too sycophantic. He does not yet realise how familiar the phrases will become.

"Good boy. Very good. Now, where on earth is Danny with…"

A knock on the door interrupts her.

"Finally! Come in."

The door is opened by a young man carrying a large silver tray. The first thing Simon notices is the man's dreadlocks, honey coloured and messily swinging behind him with every movement. His face is angular – not attractive as such, but rather possessing an unusual hollowness which draws the attention. He has freckles across the bridge of his nose and out along his cheekbones. His eyes are golden brown, like a lion's. He wears nothing but a pair of baggy cargo pants, tied at the waist and looking like they might slip off his bony hips at any moment. His nipples are large and brown. Small curls of brown hair spread between them, and down in a line past his stomach, into the low waistband of his shorts.

"Sorry, Mistress. I thought you'd want them warmed." His voice is quiet, with a rasp. He pays attention only to Alannah, ignoring Simon completely.

"Fine, just put the tray on the bed please Danny."

He nods, and carefully lowers the platter, watching that none of the items topple over. He has an easy grace about the way he moves. The stacked teacups clink but do not fall as he releases the weight of the tray onto the bed. Only the tallest item, a vase containing a single white rose, wobbles as Danny lets go of the handles. Deftly, he stills the motion with one hand, then steps back.

"Thank you, Danny. You may go."

"Thank you, Mistress." He glides out of the room as easily as he came in. Underneath his swaying dreadlocks, his back is dappled with purple-black bruises.

Thirteen

Clean

Simon's nostrils are full of the smell of warm croissants. His stomach grumbles with hunger, but his mind churns around the idea of this Danny. He is obviously a submissive. Is he Mistress' boyfriend? He didn't seem to mind her having another man in the house. Maybe she does this a lot? One thing is certain, he took a beating or two recently. Just like that man on the X-shaped cross at the ball. Simon starts to doubt Mistress' reassurances. Can he trust her not to hurt him badly? If she does, will he care or will she somehow persuade him to enjoy it? Was this how it started for Danny? Is this how he will begin to be enslaved?

Mistress pours the tea, and removes the cloth covering the pastries. She hands Simon a plate and gestures to the tray.

"Do you like strawberry jam, Simon? It's homemade.

There is something rather disappointing about bad jam, don't you think? This is delicious; Danny has a real gift in the kitchen. You should try it. He has spoilt me, I'm afraid. I can't stand the factory made stuff any more."

She dips a knife into the pot, smearing the red juice over one corner of her croissant. Simon does the same, wondering why the thought of Danny makes him uncomfortable. It doesn't feel quite like jealousy. Simon isn't stupid enough to imagine that Mistress has no other servants. No, it's something else. Maybe it's how comfortable he seemed receiving such scant praise for all this effort. Maybe it's the way his matted hair and half-nakedness made him seem more like a trained animal than a person. Or the way he didn't seem to mind being treated like one – obedient with no trace of enjoyment. He just seemed to expect it.

Simon's hunger wins out, and he occupies his mouth with food until the time seems right to ask questions. It is only when Mistress sips her second cup of tea that he brings it up.

"Have you had Danny long, Mistress? If I'm allowed to ask?"

"Oh, he's been here longer than I have. Why?"

Simon is surprised. "Longer than you? But how… isn't he your slave?"

She laughs. "Oh goodness, no! He's not mine. He's one of Richard's."

Richard. Simon frowns. Not the Master who bought him in the auction last night? The one described as a major sadist with live in-slaves. It begins to makes sense…

but if Danny belongs to Master Richard, and Danny lives here… then how does Mistress fit in? Simon recalls the dynamics between her and the Master last night. He was apologising to her. She let him kiss her. Perhaps… Simon's disgust shows on his face.

"So, you and Master Richard are…?"

Mistress Alannah raises her eyebrows. "You didn't know? Who do you think I slept with last night? Richard and I are married. We live here with two of his slaves, Sarah and Danny. There are others, sometimes. You are one of them."

Simon nods, but remains horrified. He opens his mouth before he engages his brain. "But, if you're dominant… and he's dominant…"

She cuts him off. "Oh Goodness. If I had a pound for every time I heard that question! It's none of your concern, Simon. We don't share submissives, and we don't do threesomes – at least not with each other. You don't need to know who is on top. So please keep whatever sordid things you are imagining to yourself. Now, if you've finished your breakfast, I think it's time you got in the shower."

*

Alannah collects the key from the dressing table and unlocks the ankle restraint. She is not yet convinced she can completely trust Simon to obey the proper etiquette, but she feels secure knowing that one shout would bring Richard, Danny or Sarah bounding up the staircase, should the need arise. It makes her feel a little less reckless for bringing a stranger into their home.

In the en-suite bathroom, she turns on the shower. It jets into the bathtub below, making the familiar 'tsshh' sound. White noise muffles everything outside, creating a sense of cosy intimacy. She dips her hand into the water and waits for the temperature to stabilise. When it does, she leans through the doorway and beckons Simon.

"Come on then, in you go."

The boy slides his legs out from the bed and stands up. His shoulders are hunched over, and his hands are cupped in front of his body, attempting to hide his genitals. His coyness is endearing. The sweet thing has no idea how little interest she has in his cock. He will soon learn that pleasing his Mistress should be his highest calling. Right now, it pleases her to wash her slave, so that is what they will do.

Simon approaches tentatively, checking her expression constantly for signs of displeasure. That is a good sign. He will learn quickly. She gives him an encouraging smile. He lifts one leg over the side of the bath then steps in. He is taller than she remembers from last night. Wearing boots with platform soles can give the impression that everyone else has shrunk a few inches.

"Good boy. Now, kneel down."

He complies. He moves slower than he should, but it is acceptable for now. Alannah picks the shower head from its holder. She is going to get wet, but it can't be avoided if she wants to clean him properly. She checks the water temperature one last time.

"I am going to wash you – your hair and your whole body. Do you remember the safe word to use if you don't like how I touch you?"

"Yes Mistress. I just say 'stop.'"

"That's right. Do you have any allergies or skin problems I need to know about?"

"No, Mistress."

"Good. Then put your hands on the side of the bath, spread your legs wide, and close your eyes."

He rests his hands on either side of the bath lip, and pushes his knees to the outside edge of the tub, revealing the tight curls of hair surrounding the pale lump of flesh between his legs. His breath is speeding up already, and he licks his lips as he shuts his eyes. So it wasn't just the alcohol last night – he remains very excitable.

She splashes the jet of water onto one thigh, then the other, before sliding it up onto his stomach. He catches his breath as the warm water runs down over his crotch, dripping off his balls which hang in the space between his legs. She holds the shower still for a moment, watching his hands grip the bath a little harder as his cock begins to swell and rise.

She slides the water higher, onto his chest and across each nipple, before wetting his shoulders. His lips are still open, and a mischievous thought crosses her mind. Impulsively she sprays his face, holding the shower head directly in front of his eyes and nose. Water bubbles into his nostrils and mouth, until he splutters and turns his head aside, gasping.

With a giggle, she moves the flow above his head,

drenching his hair and turning it from gold to dull brown. He blinks his eyes open and looks at her... is that hurt or confusion? Awwwh, he didn't like the water in his face. Good to know... although she did promise not to be too cruel.

"Eyes closed, Simon. That was just a little warning to close your mouth. I'm not going to drown you."

He does as she asks, leaning his head back a little to help the water flow down his back and away from his face. Good. Slowly, she trails the water jet down the length of his hair, up to his neck again and across the back of each shoulder. She slides it all the way down his spine to his buttocks, holding the jet close to his body as she works down the back of each thigh. Finally, she wets his calves and feet, which lie flush against the floor of bath beneath him. He does not flinch as the water hits his feet – not ticklish then.

She returns the jet to his chest, lifting one of his hands from the side of the bath and guiding it towards the shower head.

"Hold this here. Good boy."

He doesn't try to move or open his eyes, though he must be wondering what she is planning next. His obedience pleases her, and she makes a mental note to give him some small reward later. She reaches for the shampoo.

Alannah pours a generous palm-full of liquid and lathers it through his hair. Taking the shower head from his hand again, she rinses the bubbles down Simon's back, letting them slide over his skin and swirl down the plughole. She returns the shower head to his hand, then smooths thick conditioner through his hair. Once she is satisfied that every lock is smothered she rinses her hands in the stream of water, and reaches for a large sponge.

"That's your hair fixed. Now I am going to wash your body. Is that OK, Simon?"

"Yes, Mistress." His voice is shakes as he replies, implying he is more aroused than she realised. She looks down. Yes, his cock is hard and erect, his balls tight against his body. Damn, he really is too eager. But he is behaving himself, so there is no need to reconsider giving him a good soaping.

She covers the sponge in shower gel, rubbing it with her hand until it begins to foam. She replaces the shower head in its holder. The water will spray further now, but it will allow her more flexibility with the slave's position. She resigns herself to the sleeves of her dressing gown becoming sodden.

Leaning over, she places the sponge on the back of his shoulder, and begins to make small circles. As the foam rises, she uses her free hand to stroke along the length of each muscle, from spine to shoulder, shoulder blade to waist, lower back to hip. Circle, circle, stroke. Circle, circle, rub. Simon remains silent, but his body is tense. His fingers grip the enamel as if they are the only things tethering him to reality. His eyes are still closed, his chin thrust slightly forward and his head tilted back. He leans into every touch.

She smooths the sponge round and round, over his buttocks and down the back of his legs, pressing harder into the surface of his body now. Her left hand floats over the curve of his ass, down his legs, and back up between them. As her fingers reach the top, Simon lets out a tiny moan. It is almost inaudible, such a delicate, beautiful sound.

Alannah purrs, and slips her fingers further up, pressing firmly against the taught flesh behind Simon's balls, then sliding backwards, inching upward until they find his asshole. Simon lets out a gasp, but stays still, allowing her to massage her finger over the puckered flesh. His fingers grasp the edge of the bath so tightly that his knuckles turn white. His cock twitches, the head turning a desperate red.

That confirms it. No, this will not do. Not at all. He is too turned on to sit still for his hair brushing. He will squirm and twist and his mind will be full of plans of how to rub his cock against anything or anyone, until he is allowed to ejaculate. That would be inconvenient, and inconvenience displeases her; she wants him motionless for the next stage of her plan. And he has been rather good. He deserves a small reward. She decides to take pity on him.

She moves her left hand to the back of his neck, holding firmly. She places the sponge against his breastbone, recommencing her circles and dripping bubbles down his torso into the curled hairs below his waist. Round and round, she lathers foam across his chest, his abdomen, his groin, his legs, and back up again.

Simon's mouth is open again, making little "Oh" sounds as he breathes. He writhes his hips, attempting to push his cock towards every touch. Pinching her left hand tightly at the back of his neck, she drops the sponge and firmly grabs his shaft with her right, quickly pumping her fist along the length. He moans and leans his weight back against her supporting hand, as soap bubbles and warm water drip down his front. Fuelled by yesterday's denial, his excitement escalates rapidly. He thrusts one, twice, three times into her fist and erupts into the spurt of an orgasm. Semen shoots upwards, over Simon's head, hitting the wall next to them. Alannah laughs.

"Oh, you sweet thing. You really do have your kink muddled up with sex, don't you? Well, at least that will keep you calm for a while."

Simon's legs are shaking. He cannot reply. Tentatively, he lowers himself down to sit on his heels, his heart thudding in his chest. Mistress still holds the back of his neck with one hand. He looks up at her with a mixture of shame and awe.

"That was… Oh, God. That was…Thank you, Mistress." His face is still flushed.

Alannah smiles benevolently down at her new toy.

"Good boy. Now let's get you rinsed off."

Fourteen

Failed protection

_____

Alannah dries her slave roughly with a towel, then wraps a second one around his head. Still floating on endorphins, Simon is ushered back into the bedroom. She arranges him on the floor, settling on the stool behind him. On the dressing table lays a hairdryer, a bottle of oil, and the brush from last night.

She sighs, relaxing into the task ahead. She places her hands on his head and rubs the towel gently, discarding it to one side and picking up the brush. Switching on the hairdryer, she works slowly and methodically to dry and smooth, dry and smooth. Time seems to slow as she conducts a calming pattern with her brush, each stroke enveloping them in hot damp air, tugging and releasing on Simon's scalp, a lullaby of tingling sensations over his head and down his spine. The boy sits very still, passive and subdued. No longer full of his rutting desperation, the orgasm she bestowed has tamed her pet.

After a while, the damp brown colour lifts back to gold, and Alannah decides it is time for the oil. She rocks the switch to silence the hairdryer, and lays it on the counter. As the sound of the dryer fades a quieter buzz remains, pulsing from the bag in the corner of the room. Alannah groans, irritated.

"I should have turned that off when you mentioned it this morning." She stands and strides to the bag, unzipping pockets until she finds the offending item. She dismisses the call.

"Pin?"

Simon looks uncomfortable, but concedes his four digit code. She taps it in, making sure to stand far enough away that any sudden grab for the phone would fail.

"Fifteen missed calls. All from the same person... Kate."

Simon's jaw drops open.

"Oh, shit! Kate! I was supposed to meet her at the cloakroom last night. I forgot all about it. She's probably going crazy."

Alannah raises an eyebrow. "Well, let's see what she has to say. She left you quite a few messages."

Mistress glares at Simon, discouraging him from moving whilst she turns on the speaker and plays the series of increasingly panicked voicemails.

"Simon, it's three fifteen, where the hell are you? You won't believe the night I've had! I need to tell you EVERYTHING. Hope you had a good one too. Don't make me wait, you know I hate it."

"Simon, the bouncers made everyone leave, I'm outside the main door and its bloody freezing so hurry up and get your sorry butt over here before I get a cab without you."

"Simon, you better be gagged and bound somewhere getting fucked in the ass by your new friend because if you don't have a damn good excuse for leaving me standing on my own in the middle of the night in the freezing cold, I swear to God I am gonna kill you ten times over. Last warning before I go without you."

"Simon, where the hell are you? The bouncer said Master Richard left hours ago. There's no-one left inside, they're locking the doors. What the hell happened to you?"

"Look, I'm getting worried. Just call me. I'm going home now. I guess you hooked up with someone. I hope you're OK. We had a plan, it's not cool to just leave me hanging like that. You could've texted me or something."

"Simon, I just got home. Still nothing from you. You're freaking me out. I'm going to bed now, but call me when you get this message, OK? Even if it's the middle of the night. I hope your phone just ran out of charge or something. You're gonna be buying me drinks for weeks to make this up to me, OK?"

"Simon, it's eleven thirty. I called your flatmates, they said you didn't come home last night. I'm not gonna lie, I'm really worried right now. It's not like you to just disappear. Look, I might be panicking but I keep thinking… what if Master Richard did something to you? What if you're in trouble? I'm going to wait a few more hours then call the police."

"Bloody hell, Simon, still nothing. If you just passed out drunk on a night bus, you would be home by now. I can't shake the feeling that something awful has happened. I'll give it another hour, then I'm calling the police. So ring me right now, you hear? Cos if you just broke your phone or managed to pull someone… Look, if I have to call the police and explain where we were last night, I swear… you'd best be dying in a ditch somewhere or I'm gonna make the rest of your life so bloody miserable you'll wish Master Richard had got hold of you instead. I'm freaking out here. I hope I'm wrong. Maybe there is some lame explanation. But I can't just sit here and do nothing, when he might have… Well, just call me, OK?"

Police. The venue for the club, together with Richard's name, will bring them straight to the house. Alannah presses her lips together in annoyance.

Simon breaks the silence first.

"Oh God, she sounds mad. Please, Mistress, can I call her back? I completely forgot I was supposed to meet her. I'm sorry. It won't take long."

She is angrier than he thought.

"You stupid boy. You arranged a check in and you forgot about it? Really?"

"A check in? We were just going to meet up and travel home together."

"You arranged to meet at the end of the evening?"

"Yes."

"And when you didn't turn up, she believed you were in danger?"

"Yeah, I guess. It's fine though, she'll calm down."

"So you failed to check in as arranged? You knew she would be concerned for your safety. And you didn't think to mention this earlier?"

"Umm... no, Mistress. I had my mind on other things. Like you." He flicks his eyes up from the floor to see whether she still looks mad. She does, and the implied flattery does not stop her lecture.

"And worse, she failed to do anything about it until the following afternoon? Idiots, the pair of you. You must never ignore safety precautions like that. Set them up and follow them, or don't set them up at all. False security is worse than no security. Safety is the first rule."

"I'm sorry, Mistress. I just didn't think. Can I call her? Please?"

"Oh, you're going to call her all right. Immediately. I don't want the police turning up on my doorstep, especially not today. You really would be in trouble with Richard!"

Simon sheepishly holds his hand out for the phone, but she shakes her head. Dialling the number, she turns the speaker back on, holding the phone out of his reach.

*

The line connects. Kate's phone barely rings before she answers.

"Simon? SIMON? Is that you?"

"Kate? Yes, it's me."

"Oh my God, where the hell are you? Are you OK? What happened?"

"I'm fine. Everything's fine. I only just got your voicemails. I'm sorry about last night."

"What the hell happened, Simon? You stood me up."

"I'm sorry. I completely forgot. Something happened…" he looks at Mistress Alannah, who gestures for him to get on with it.

"What? What happened? Did you…" he cuts her off.

"Kate, you didn't call the police, did you?"

"I was just about to, you moron. I was so bloody worried. You didn't answer your phone all night. I thought that psycho kidnapped you. I called your flatmates and everything. I was THIS close to reporting you missing. Oh my God, can you imagine? I would have died of shame. Having to explain that your friend disappeared from some fetish club? To the bloody police?"

Alannah visibly relaxes.

"I'm really sorry Kate. I'll explain later, OK?"

"Oh no, you don't get off that easily. What happened? I looked for you everywhere. Where did Master Richard take you? Did you go home with him?"

"No… well, not exactly. I'll tell you later."

"Not exactly? What does that mean?"

"Nothing. I'll explain later."

"Where are you? At home? I'm coming over."

"No, don't. I'm… look I'm not home yet, OK?"

"Oh my God, did you pull? Are you still there? Wait – you didn't sleep with Master Richard, did you? Did you let him fuck you? Oh my God, Simon, what have you done?"

"No! God, Kate, it's not like that. It's not him. He didn't lay a finger on me."

"But he bought you at the auction. What do you mean he didn't lay a finger on you?"

"Kate, I have to go."

"Is it a woman?"

Simon pauses, and Alannah raises a half smile.

"Erm… yes. But I can't talk right now."

"Why not? Who is it? Did you find a Mistress to break you in? Oh my God, Simon, did you get laid? You've got to tell me right now. You owe me, big time, remember?"

Simon looks to Mistress Alannah in embarrassment. "I really can't talk just now."

"Why not? Is she there?"

"Erm…" Simon searches for reassurance in Mistress' expression. She offers him nothing to go on.

"Simon, is she there right now? Oh my God, can she hear what you're saying?"

Alannah smiles a wry smile, and gives the smallest of nods.

"Yes."

"Shit! Simon, you should have told me! OK, so you can't say much, I get it. Full debrief later, OK? Just tell me, simple yes or no, was it good? Did you get everything you hoped for?"

"Kate, please just shut up. Just stop talking, OK?"

"Why? What do you mean?"

Simon pauses. Mistress seems amused to watch him squirm. She lets the call run on in awkward silence.

"Simon? What's wrong?"

"You're on speakerphone."

Kate shrieks, stopping only to unleash a stream of expletives.

Alannah decides the phone call is over.

"You can stop worrying about your friend now, Kate. He's quite safe. You can have him back when I'm finished with him. In the mean time, please refrain from calling the police. It is completely unnecessary, and would be highly embarrassing for all concerned. Goodbye."

She ends the call and tosses the phone back towards Simon's bag.

*

Through the uncomfortable quiet that descends Simon hears a noise in the house, several floors beneath them. It sounds like someone is moving furniture. A heavy object crashes. Someone screams.

Simon eyes the door suspiciously.

"Mistress? Should we go downstairs and check everything's OK?"

She shakes her head.

"No. It's fine. Richard's working from home today. Best

not to interrupt."

More clattering, and a woman shouting something unintelligible. Simon looks bewildered. She smiles.

"Don't worry. It's a Con Non-con client. Not the easiest type of scene to explain to unexpected guests. A visit from the police would be most inconvenient."

Mistress resumes her place on the stool by the dressing table, unperturbed.

"Now come here and let me oil your hair."

Fifteen

What Mistress Desires

Alannah spends a long time stroking Simon's hair, playing with it and running her fingers down his neck. Her emotions ebb and flow as she considers the events of the last twelve hours. She is not usually this mercurial. It feels odd, and yet not uncomfortable.

Anger, still, towards Richard. That will take more time to subside. Behind that, uncertainty, generated by his unexpected reaction. Has she misjudged him? Is he less trustworthy than she thought?

No. No, it is the stress of their current circumstance which lies behind it. Poor Danny. Unreachable by conventional help, and in so much pain. He found his comfort, and it worked for a time. Now he seems to be drifting deeper, out of reach. She has no more ideas for how to help. Perhaps the shift in priorities will necessitate a more radical solution. It could get ugly.

She sighs, resting her cheek in Simon's hair for a moment, allowing her thoughts to return to last night. The tide of feelings turns again, and she smiles.

Pride swells. Amazement at the sheer nerve of him, presenting his gift in front of everyone. Respect, and deep affection. The warm feeling of being held in high esteem by the man she loves. Amusement, at his incorrigible habit for grand gestures.

And this slave... So fresh and new, but so unschooled and foolish. Half her instinct is to discard him. To reject him for his stupidity about the phone, the missed meeting with Kate, over his ridiculous and persistent desire for sex. The other half wants to train him. To gently coax him into obedience and knowing his place. To show him what it feels like to be completely filled with pleasure-pain. To give him the experience of being tamed and controlled, being overshadowed by someone stronger than himself. She wonders if he will be one of the silent ones, or a screamer. Will he beg, or curse, or just moan?

But perhaps he is too much trouble to bother with. Perhaps she will send him home and take a long bath, watch a film, start wading through her client emails.

At least for now he is being quiet. Despite his flaws, he seems eager to please and quick to learn. And the hair is... she inhales, ingesting the scent of oil and shampoo... yes, the hair is almost perfect. There is something calming about it. And his trespasses are easily managed. Better to have an innocent one hoping for sex than an experienced one listing a precise schematic for their ideal scene. This one is more... malleable.

She digs her thumbs into the flesh underneath his shoulder blades, rotating in small circles upwards and inwards until she reaches his spine. He groans, arching his back slightly, then gasps air deeply. She holds the pressure until he releases the breath, then rocks her thumbs between each vertebrae until she reaches his nape.

Unexpectedly, he speaks. "Please, Mistress."

Alannah does not respond immediately, but continues to press into the gaps between each bone until her thumbs are pressed underneath the base of his skull.

"What is it, Simon?"

"Please Mistress... I want to do something for you. I want to please you, Mistress."

"You are pleasing me, Simon. You are doing exactly what I want you to do."

"I mean... I want to make you come, Mistress. You did it to me. I want to please you too. Any way you like, Mistress, with my hands, or my mouth, or..."

"No. I don't think so, Simon. If I wanted an orgasm I would take one. That is not what I want from you."

"But... Mistress, I don't get it. Doing this... doesn't it make you feel... doesn't it turn you on?"

"No, not really. It doesn't make me want the physical pleasures of genital stimulation, if that's what you mean. But it does make me hungry for other things. There are other desires beyond the mere sexual, Simon."

"I don't understand, Mistress."

"That's because you are green, and ignorant, and in need of training, Simon."

"I'm sorry Mistress. I just… please, tell me what you want."

"Very well. Perhaps you need a little more verbal encouragement than I've been giving you. That's fine. I can talk you through our play as we go." She twists one hand into his hair, grabbing and pulling backwards until his head rests on her body. She slips the other hand under his arm, pushing her palm flat on his solar plexus, holding him against her. She whispers into the top of his head.

"I wanted to play with your hair. I wanted to wash it and dry it, oil it and run my hands through it. You have been very good whilst I took what I wanted. And now I've had enough of your hair, Simon. Now, I want something more. Now, I want to hurt you."

He shivers.

"Remember what we talked about last night, Simon? About the crop? And the violet wand?"

Simon tries to nod, but he can't move his head. "I'm scared, Mistress. I want to, but I'm scared."

Alannah smiles, releasing her hand from his chest, pulling his head further back so his throat protrudes, exposed. Gently, she places two fingers against his jugular, feeling his pulse.

"I'll go slowly. I'll be very careful with you." She leans down as if to kiss his neck, but instead licks down the length of his carotid artery, from jawline to the hollow beneath his larynx.

"Nothing without your consent, Simon. You can use your safe word to stop it at any point. But if you really want to please me…" This time she does kiss his neck, softly feathering her lips across the warm skin, stopping just behind his ear. She whispers, "If you really want to please me, Simon, this is the only way."

The slave opens his eyes, straining to look at her in the corner of his field of vision. She smiles warmly, or at least attempts to. It doesn't quite conceal the cold hard hunger growing in her heart. She sighs, dips her lashes, and pushes to close.

"Isn't this what you wanted, Simon?"

Too easy, perhaps, but the victory is still sweet.

"OK. I'll try, Mistress. I do want to please you. I'll try my best."

She laughs, throwing his head away from her body so that he overbalances, landing on the floor on all fours.

"Good boy. Now, I wonder if Richard has finished with the dungeon?"

*

Simon narrowly escapes banging his nose on the floor as Mistress pushes him forward. He picks himself back up into a kneeling position, and sees that Mistress has his collar in her hand. She threads it around his neck, fastening the buckle and arranging it so the rope hangs in the front.

Only then does the adrenaline wash over him. Dungeon. Oh Christ, she is taking him to the dungeon. What has he agreed to?

"Come on," she says cheerfully, as if this is a perfectly normal situation to be in. Simon scrabbles to his feet. As he stands, he has the presence of mind to grab a towel to wrap around his waist. At least he won't be paraded through the house naked.

She leads him out of the room and down the stairs. One floor down, a door is open. Behind a desk, Master Richard reclines in a chair. His hair is loose, and his shirt unbuttoned. His lip is split open, bleeding. Alannah stops.

"Good session?"

"Very satisfactory, thank you. Tight and wet in all the right places."

"Looks like she put up quite a fight?"

He smiles, and licks the blood from his lip. "This? Yes, she was quite feisty. But you should see the other girl."

"Oh dear, poor Sarah. Anything needing medical attention?"

"No, I don't think so. Nothing a little ice won't fix."

"Glad to hear it."

"Is your gift behaving himself?" Richard's eyes freeze into Simon just long enough to ignite terror.

"He's doing all right… so far. For a beginner."

"Well, if you want any help breaking him in, I'd be happy to oblige." Simon's blood runs cold at the suggestion.

"Oh, Richard, so soon? It can't have been such a good session if you're already craving the next one."

"I'm a professional. I can be ready. Just give me an hour…" he glances down at his crotch, then shakes his head. "… fine, maybe two." She laughs, but Simon isn't finding this funny at all.

"Is the dungeon free? Everything cleaned up?"

"Yes, it should be. She ought to be finished by now."

"Good. Our turn then. See you later my love."

"Have fun."

*

Mistress leads Simon down another flight to the ground floor. As they turn the corner they come face to face with a silver tray, being carried by a short round woman. On the tray is a bottle of whiskey, a cut glass tumbler, a bucket of ice, and a cloth napkin. The woman's dirty blonde hair is cut in a long bob. She is dressed, if it could be called that, in nothing but a white apron, edged in frills and reaching down to her plump thighs. The material barely covers her breasts, which lay heavy and low, bulging out from the sides of the narrow bib. Her nipples are clearly visible underneath.

Simon tries not to gawp, but manages only to shift the focus of his stare upwards. The whole left side of her face is red and swollen. Her eye is half closed, and there is dried blood by her ear. She looks like she's gone a couple of rounds in a boxing ring.

Mistress steps back against the wall to let her past, pushing Simon to do the same.

"Thank you, Mistress."

"Did you enjoy yourself, Sarah?"

"Master said I was a good girl, Mistress."

"Of course you were. Is that a black eye coming up, Sarah?"

The beaten woman gives a filthy smile. "I hope so, Mistress."

"He'll like that. You will be popular for the next few days."

"Whatever Master wants, Mistress."

"Good girl. Up you go now, don't keep him waiting. She must have paid well if he's drinking the good stuff."

"Yes, Mistress."

She climbs the stairs, leaving Simon struggling not to watch her naked ass as she plods upwards. Although he tries not to look, he can't help noticing something is very wrong with her back. The skin is criss-crossed with silvery scars. Among them, fresh red lines, reaching down the back of her legs, where they give way to darker splodges of black bruise. One mark stands out amongst the others, an ugly red-purple circle at the back of her right shoulder. Her body is a mess.

Mistress Alannah tugs on his leash, bringing his attention back to where it should have been.

"Do we have a problem, Simon?"

Slowly, Simon shakes his head. "No, Mistress. No problem."

Mistress nods. "Good. Come on then."

A few steps down the hall, Mistress pushes on the hidden panel under the stairs. The door clicks open. A dark staircase twists downwards. At the bottom, a dim light shines on a heavy velvet curtain, shrouding the room beyond from view.

Mistress holds the door open, and gestures below.

"After you."

Hesitantly, Simon steps into the gloom.

Sixteen

The Dungeon

Simon descends the steps tentatively, trailing his hand down the bannister as if he expects the staircase to buck and throw him off. Mistress follows silently behind him. Reaching the bottom, he pushes the curtain aside and steps into the dungeon.

It is brighter than he imagined. Warmer, too. White walls and a pale stone floor. Simon isn't exactly sure what he expected, but it isn't the feeling of space and air which this room possesses. It has a minimalist feel, or more accurately one of straightforward practicality. No pictures on the walls, no ornamental light fittings, in fact, no decoration at all. The room is furnished with function, not beauty, in mind.

Across from Simon, and dominating the right side of the space, stands a large St Andrew's cross. Seven feet high with padded black leather and metal rings, it eats the light and malevolently nurses its secrets. To the left, a smaller bench stands on the floor. It has two flat leather surfaces at different heights, and two of its legs are padded. Every corner is adorned with metal restraint rings, or square tubes for inserting worse attachments. On the wall behind, next to another door, a heavy chain hangs from a fitting embedded in the masonry. The wall behind the chain is covered with a clear perspex screen, and something resembling a shower tray covers the floor below.

Movement attracts Simon's attention upward. The lights are simple spots, set within and scattered across the whole ceiling. Between them hang loops, big steel circles dangling from smaller structures fixed within the roof. He counts twelve, symmetrically spanning the centre of the room in three rows. Each hoop has a narrow string hanging from it and swaying gently from the motion of the air. Every string ends with a loose knot, dangling down just above head height.

Next to the St Andrew's cross, against the opposite wall, there is an iron cage. Four feet high, with heavy bars and ugly welding, it is clearly not here for its aesthetic. The padlock on the door is shiny brass. It gleams in the light, out of place with the black leather and dark metal elsewhere.

He expects to find a wall adjacent to the staircase door, but none exists. Instead the room stretches on behind them, double sized and running under the whole length of the house. He turns towards the far end. There is a comfortable looking sofa, and a pair of simple chairs. Almost cosy. There is even a rug on the floor. A table bears a kettle and cups. A tall bookcase holds folded towels and something which might be blankets. There is a sink with a vanity unit. On the top stands a bright yellow sharps box. A high window, perhaps looking up into the garden, blanked with frosted glass.

Filling the last space, flush against the wall of the stairwell, is an enormous cabinet. Double folding doors sit menacingly shut, their heavy handles daring to be pulled open. Two deep drawers squat beneath. On the side facing Simon are three small hooks, all empty. Two feet down, an arc scratched in the wood below hints silently at a missing object habitually hung there.

As he turns full circle, Simon comes back to face Mistress Alannah. She is leaning against the door frame, waiting for him to take in his surroundings.

"Not too scary, I hope?"

He shakes his head, not in agreement but because it is expected.

"Well, let's see what toys we might play with."

Mistress strides over to the cabinet. She looks small next to the imposing wooden hulk. Simon wonders if she will struggle to move the heavy doors, but she tugs unceremoniously on the handles and the doors glide open easily, each one folding back on itself down the centre, forming neat flanks to frame the space within. Mistress beckons to him and Simon creeps closer until he can see the contents clearly.

At first glance, the inside looks like a wardrobe. On the left, several hanging rails run front to back. Instead of clothes, long slender implements hang down. Slim lines of black leather, stiff wood and brightly coloured rubber. All manner of whips, canes and floggers, each one suspended from the rails in a dense thicket of threats. On the right are shelves. At eye level are two large baskets, contents unknown, each marked with a name: Sarah; Danny. A broad shelf across the top of the cabinet holds boxes, unmarked or bearing simple logos which reveal no clues about their innards. Lower shelves hold smaller baskets which Simon can see into. Their contents are recognisable; metal clamps, karabiners, padlocks, condoms, sachets of lube, boxes of thin needles. One holds a myriad of tiny bullet vibrators. Another has folded sheets of latex, a funnel and a rubber hose.

Mistress Alannah bends down, and heaves open one of the low drawers underneath. It is divided into neat compartments, each containing its own stock. These are larger items than on the shelves above: ropes, lengths of chain, cuffs made of leather and of metal, a curled bullwhip, ball gags, harnesses, and a selection of dildos and vibrators, mostly still in their packaging.

Mistress turns to face Simon and puts her hands on her hips.

"So, where shall we start?"

Simon's eyes keep returning to the stack of dildos. There is a black rubber butt plug on the top of the pile, tapered in a diamond shape and ending in a solid flat circle. He clenches his buttocks.

"Do you like them?" Mistress has noticed.

"No, Mistress. I don't want anything up my ass. No, thanks."

"Awwh, that's a shame. How about in your mouth?"

Simon shakes his head vigorously.

"Oh well, never mind. No need to look so worried. I won't do anything without your consent. There are lots of other things we can try. But it's not going to work unless you trust me. Are you afraid I'm going to ignore your boundaries?"

Simon isn't certain, but his dick is already throbbing, and he desperately wants to take things further. Even though she is terrifying, something about being out of his depth turns him on. He confesses eagerly.

"I trust you, Mistress. I'm just a bit scared. But I do want to try."

"Good boy. Well, how about we start with some of these?" She reaches into the drawer and pulls out two leather cuffs, lined in sheepskin. They are lumpy, heavy things.

"...and one of these?" She reaches into the forest of sticks and selects a black riding crop. "I would like to tie you to the bench and teach you how to take it. Like we discussed upstairs?"

Simon stares at the crop, feeling the air fill his lungs then seep out. Rise, and fall. Underneath, the tap, tap, tap of his heart gets faster. He takes his decision.

"OK." He sounds more nervous than he feels. He walks over to the bench, and offers his wrists, palms upward, for the restraints. "So, how am I supposed to get on this thing?"

When Mistress doesn't reply, he turns back to see that she still stands by the cabinet. She has her hand over her mouth, hiding a grin.

"Oh, sweetheart."

Another fuck up. What did he do wrong this time? He hates being laughed at. Hurt, he shrugs and spits out "What?"

She sighs in frustration. "What… Mistress?"

He looks at the floor, repeating "What, Mistress?"

"Better." She shakes her head. "I like that you're eager, Simon, I really do. But we are not ready for the bench just yet. You should always wait until you're instructed to use the equipment."

He nods, sadly. "Sorry, Mistress."

"Please don't get upset, Simon. You have a lot to learn, but there's no shame in that. Everyone has to start at the beginning. You just need to pay attention to your attitude. I will teach you the rest. If you'll let me. Stop pushing and let me take control."

Simon's anger dissolves, replaced with surging desire. Yes, he wants her to teach him. He would do almost anything to have this woman tie him up and touch him. Even let her hurt him. He's just got to keep his head and try not to make more mistakes.

"I'm sorry, Mistress. Sorry I keep getting it wrong. I do want you to teach me, please Mistress. I promise I'll try my best." He shifts, uncomfortably.

"Good boy. See, you're learning already. You'll do fine. To be honest, I rather like the fact that you're so green. It's been a long time since I've schooled someone as new as you."

Simon looks up through furrowed brows. "Really, Mistress? I thought I was annoying you?"

"A little, perhaps. Almost all submissives annoy me at some point during a scene. At least you won't have picked up too many bad habits – yet. And it's such a special thing to do – to show someone the ways into the deep, intense spaces within the mind. Spaces where you can come adrift from normal reality, and where the only thing that exists is the current sensation and how to weather it. That, and the security of knowing that your Top will bring you safely back out the other side. It's a very powerful place, and it changes people. It can even be addictive. Really entering into it takes time and patience, and a lot of trust. We won't get that far today, but I can start you on the path towards it."

"Is that really how it feels, Mistress?" Simon asks, optimistically.

"Yes. At least, so I'm told."

"Told, Mistress? Isn't that how you feel?"

"No. It's different for the Dominant. You have to remain aware of what's going on and how your play partner is doing. There is a lot of responsibility. It can still be overwhelming, sometimes, and of course it's very enjoyable. But it's not a letting go. It's more about the rush of taking control. Knowing you've been trusted with the most intimate parts of someone's soul and proving yourself worthy of that trust. I aim to take my submissives just outside their comfort zone. Not so far that they safeword out and rescind consent – that would mean I've badly misread them – but far enough into jeopardy that they relinquish any fiction of having agency over the situation. And afterwards, when they have experienced being utterly out of control, I slowly hand back the reins and restore their autonomy. It's a beautiful thing, when it goes well. Nothing interests me more than a person who wants to offer themselves to me like that."

The longing Simon feels to be part of this beautiful thing is painful.

"I think you've just described something I've always wanted, but couldn't express. Please, Mistress, would you do that to me?"

Mistress Alannah stares at him for too long, before breaking into a predatory smile.

"Simon, I think you're flirting with me."

Simon doesn't know if that's a good thing or a bad thing. Is it allowed?

"I don't mean to be disrespectful. I just thought… I thought what you said sounds amazing, and I'd really like to try it. If that's OK, Mistress?"

Alannah bites her lip, and turns her head to one side. She takes a deep breath, puts one hand on her hip, and exhales slowly before looking at Simon again.

"Yes, it's OK, Simon. I'm glad you want to try it. It would be an honour to help you. Now come and sit with me, so we can agree exactly what we are going to do."

Seventeen

It's going to hurt

Mistress Alannah glides over to the sofa and sits down, placing the cuffs and the crop on the table before her. Simon follows. Remembering that he shouldn't sit on the chairs, he stops short, waiting awkwardly for direction.

Mistress looks pleased. "Good boy, Simon. You may come and sit on the rug."

Simon obeys quickly, crossing his legs to sit before realising there is no way to do it modestly whilst only wearing a towel. He tells himself it doesn't matter. She's already seen him naked, and he's about to let her tie him up and whip him. There is no point getting shy about his balls hanging down below the gaping cloth. Mistress doesn't even seem to notice. She clasps her hands in her lap, and leans towards him.

"So… Have you done this before?" She nods towards the table. "Taken a beating?"

He shakes his head. "No, Mistress."

"That's OK. I will teach you." She pauses for a moment. "First we need to decide how hard we are going to play. There are a few different techniques, but let's keep things simple. I could work fast and light, like we talked about last night. That means we would focus more on the idea of being restrained and disciplined, rather than the physical sensation. If that's all you want, that's absolutely fine. It's a completely valid scene... for a beginner. Or, we could try something that will make better use of my skills. I could take you on a deeper path, perhaps even into subspace. But for that, I would have to hit you. Really hit you."

Simon frowns. He knows she is manipulating him, but he still wants her approval. If he turns down the wilder adventure, he will regret it later. But he is afraid of giving her free reign to hurt him.

"I'm not sure, Mistress. What if it's too much for me? I don't want to start something then disappoint you."

"That's why we will have frequent check ins. And you have your safe word. If you ever need to use it, I will be much more disappointed in myself than in you, Simon."

"You would?"

"I would. Everyone has a different pain tolerance. Very few people actually enjoy the pain itself. Most subs endure it because of the effect it creates. It's not about how much pain you can take. It's about giving me the responsibility for steering you through the pain, and trusting me to find the right balance – enough to cause the feeling we are looking for, but not so much that you can't bear it."

"No offense, Mistress, but how will you know if it's

hurting me too much?" Simon watches carefully for signs he's overstepped the mark, but Mistress shows no indication of irritation. She explains with patience.

"That's what the check ins are for. We will use a traffic light system. I will ask you to give me a colour. You will say 'green', 'orange' or 'red'. If you like what we're doing and want to keep going, you say 'green'. If the intensity is a little high but you're still coping, you say 'orange'. 'Red' means you're past your limit and you can't continue at that level. The colours are a simple way for you to express how you're feeling. They are not a way for you direct what happens – I will still be in control. I might choose to push you further after you've said 'orange', or even 'red'. The more I get to know someone, the more comfortable I am pushing their boundaries and being a better judge than they are about what they can take. I doubt I'll push you too hard today, as we are new to one another. But if I do, and you don't want to carry on; if you panic, or if you need me to stop for any other reason, that's when you use your safe word. You can say 'stop' at any time, and I will immediately end the scene. I might ignore your 'red' but I will never ignore your 'stop'. Safe words are absolutely sacred, they should always be respected."

She lets her words sink in before continuing. "Does that make sense? Do you have any questions? Are there any parts which you don't understand?"

A warm sense of anticipation spreads through Simon's belly. It does make sense. He'll have a way out if he needs it. But apart from that one escape route, he will be completely at her mercy. He imagines himself saying 'orange' and being ignored, and the tingles grow, spreading out from his core down the inside of his arms, fluttering like moths against the heels of his hands. He wants this so badly.

He nods, positively. "Yes, Mistress. It makes sense. Thank you for explaining it."

"Good boy, Simon. Very good. Next, we should talk about the pain. It's better if you know what's going to happen. Do you know how it works?"

He is frustrated there is more to discuss. He is eager to feel her touch him, even eager to feel the crop on his flesh. He doesn't want to think about the pain. He wants to let her worry about that. He wants to focus only on trying his best, on being her good boy.

"No, Mistress."

"It's going to hurt. If you know to expect it, you're less likely to panic. To start with it's going to feel quite bearable, but the pain will build up quickly and it will begin to hurt a lot. After a few minutes you'll reach a point where you'll feel like you can't carry on. When you get there, I need you to tell me. I don't want you to hide how you're feeling – that will not please me at all. Honesty, obedience and consent are the principles we live by in this house. When you reach that point, I'm not going to stop, not unless you use your safe word. But I will reduce the intensity for a while. When you get there, you need to keep breathing and wait for your endorphins to kick in. You can remind yourself that you can trust me, and that you have got your safe word if you need it. You can think about how much you want to please me. You have to go through this stage before you get to the next one. "

Simon is appalled, but manages to respond. "Umm, OK."

"After that, we get to the good part. People describe it in different ways. Some say they feel high, and that the pain goes out of focus so that it doesn't hurt as much even though it's still there. Others talk about a feeling of being underwater or covered by a heavy duvet, a sense of being comforted and shielded from the pain. It's really your neurochemistry reacting to alter your perception of reality. It's a survival instinct. A deeply ingrained defence mechanism that protects you from being overwhelmed by your pain for long enough to escape whatever deadly situation you're in and reach safety. A little like fight or flight, but with endorphins instead of adrenaline. We are going to take advantage of that defence mechanism to help you experience the euphoria without actually damaging your body."

"We will use physical restraint to heighten the sense of danger, and to trigger your association between bondage, sexuality and pleasure. We are going to create a glorious mix of dopamine, oxytocin and serotonin inside your brain to float you into bliss. How does that sound, Simon?"

How can he convey how good that sounds? Simon suspects she sees it in his face. She can certainly see the bulge under the towel. He stutters out a few words, but the message is carried by his eyes, gazing up at her with his pupils wide in expectation.

"Good boy. I'm sure you'll do just fine. I will keep you in that space for a while. Half an hour will be long enough, to begin with. The way you experience time might change, so it might feel a lot longer than that, or it might seem over very quickly. Afterwards, you will probably feel strange. There can be a come down. Sometimes it happens immediately, sometimes days later. You might feel cold and shaky, or very emotional. Some people get tearful, others experience strong feelings of guilt. That's normal, and I will help you through it. After I've finished playing with you, we will sit together here on the sofa whilst you recover. I will take care of you until you've levelled out and feel better. Do you understand?"

"Yes, Mistress."

"Do you have any questions?"

"No, Mistress."

"Are you sure? This is your last opportunity before we begin. There are no silly questions, it's always better to double check if you have any doubt at all."

Simon does not want to wait any longer, he wants to feel the cuffs on his wrists and the cool leather of the bench beneath him. But one nagging thought remains. Has she forgotten?

"Well… I do have one question, Mistress. What about the violet wand? Will we do that afterwards?"

She looks at him, amused.

"Let's not be over ambitious for your first real scene, Simon."

"Yes, Mistress. But… "

"But what, Simon?"

"Sorry, Mistress… but isn't that why you brought me back to your house? Because you didn't have a violet wand at the ball?"

She laughs, then tries to suppress it.

"Oh, Simon. There's no need for either of us to stand on that pretence any more. We both had other motives, there's no shame in admitting them."

He looks uncertain. "We did, Mistress?"

"Yes, of course we did. I was tired, as I told you last night. I needed to sleep before I could enjoy you properly. And your hair needed washing. But mostly, I wanted to see if I could do it. To persuade a complete stranger to get in my car and come home with me. That wouldn't have meant much from a hard-core fetishist who knew what to expect, but persuading a fresh green newbie – well, that felt like a challenge. I was rather pleased to find I could."

Simon does not find her words reassuring. She carries on.

"You were too nervous to enjoy a scene in front of a full playroom. You wanted more privacy. You hoped that coming home with me meant I would spend more time playing with you. I practically promised you that much. You wanted to see whether the great Mistress Alannah lived up to the hype. You were flattered I even asked you. And, despite the fact I was very clear with you, you still hoped that being here overnight meant you had a chance of fucking me."

How could she see inside his skull like that? "I… I don't know what to say, Mistress."

"Are you going to deny it?"

Simon squeezes his eyes shut and cringes. He shakes his head. "No, Mistress, I guess not."

Her hand stroking his face startles him. She places a

finger under his chin, and tilts his face up towards her.

"Well, at least you got one orgasm out of it. And if you are a very, very good boy, Simon… if you take the crop well, I might let you have another. But no promises."

Simon blushes, lost for words to express the flood of sudden desire he feels. Tongue tied, he returns to the previous subject.

"So, does that mean we're not going to play with the violet wand, Mistress?"

She rolls her eyes. "You're very persistent, aren't you Simon? Well, how about this – I'll assess how you're doing after the crop. If I think you can take it, and you still want to try, I'll introduce you to the wand. But there's every chance you'll have had enough by then. If I don't think it's safe to continue, no wand. Deal?"

"Deal, Mistress. Thank you."

"Good. Now, I think it's high time I took you to the bench, don't you?"

A final surge of panic passes quickly enough for Simon to reply. "Yes please, Mistress."

"Wrists."

Simon stretches his arms out towards her. Mistress picks up one heavy cuff, wrapping it from the inside to the outside of his arm, and closing the fastening at the back, where it is hardest to reach. The second follows. Underneath the leather, the sheepskin presses firmly but does not constrict.

Mistress smiles approvingly, stands up, then threads her index finger through the metal D ring on each cuff, trapping his wrists together. Her hand brushes against the sensitive skin inside, and for a moment Simon can barely breathe.

"Stand up." Mistress draws his wrists upwards as he rises. Somehow, this is really happening. He is standing in a dungeon with this woman, his wrists bound, ready to be tied and whipped and everything else. It's actually happening.

"Good boy. Come with me."

Eighteen

The Bench

––––––––––––––

Alannah leads the boy to the bench, a single finger reeling him along without resistance.

She lets go of his wrists, and takes a moment to draw herself up to her full height, shoulders back, crop angled down towards the floor ready for use. After all the preparation, finally they come to this focal point. The air feels thick with it, heavy and humid like incense in an old cathedral. Spacious and intimate, holy and profane.

She looks him up and down one last time, noticing the shape of his body, the placement of his nipples, the flow of hair down his stomach growing darker as it goes lower into the towel, the lumpy curves of his knees, round calves ending with bony feet. Deliberately, she turns to look at the lower leather surface.

"Kneel."

He drops one knee, then the other, onto the black.

"Good. Now lie down."

She walks to the front of the bench as he lowers his stomach onto the higher surface. It is not quite flat; his chest rests lower than his hips. His shoulders and head project beyond the bench, unsupported. He still holds his head out stiffly. Soon he will learn to release it. She smiles.

"Good boy."

She rests one hand on his shoulder, then slides it down his arm to the cuff. Deftly, she clips the D ring to the bench leg. Standing, she circles round to repeat the process for his other wrist. He still looks calm. He shifts his weight a little as he relaxes into posture. A positive sign, but he is resting too far backwards. She moves behind the bench, stroking a hand from his shoulder down his back as she goes.

She rests her hands on his hips. Placing one knee between his legs, she leans forwards and presses herself against his ass.

"Just move a little... further... on" He tenses, then yields, wriggling away until his thighs are flush against the vertical pad.

"Better."

Now for the waist strap. She reaches under the table for the wide leather, punctured with neat rows of holes to match its double buckle. Gently, she lays it across the slave's back, threading the end loosely through before smoothing a hand between the strap and the skin, constricting it tightly, and releasing to fasten it one notch looser than the tightest place. This part always reminds her of the horses on the farm. Getting ready to ride out, fastening the girth on the saddle. Her brother teaching her how to do it; check the skin isn't trapped, wait until he breathes out, space for two fingers all the way around.

It's a long time since she's been on a horse. Aaron definitely wouldn't approve of this poor colt. And this one is not for riding, at least not today.

Time to uncover him. She grabs a handful of towel and pulls. It is difficult to remove, now that his thighs and groin are pressed hard into the bench. A few sharp tugs do the job. Simon rocks against the bench, trying to adjust the way his cock lies squashed against the surface. Already, his movement is restricted. It's sweet, seeing him uncomfortable.

Two more restraints before the next part.

Fishing out one strap from behind the vertical pad, she threads it midway across one thigh and under the other, buckling it at the far side. The second strap goes lower, closer to his knees. She is careful to leave a gap between them so they won't pinch together. Under then over, completing the figure eight, holding his legs in place. No escape now.

She stands back to assess her work. He is completely tied. Arms, waist and thighs pinned, ass in the air and those beautiful blonde waves falling to the floor in front of his face. Trapped, ready, and at her mercy. She relishes the momentary rush of excitement before concentrating again.

Safety first. His hair would sway wonderfully as he takes the crop, but she must be sensible. He is a beginner and she must be able to see his face. It must be tied, like the rest of him. She returns to the cabinet and fishes a hair band from the depths. She sweeps the boy's hair to one side, and loosely bundles it into the band. It is perfect; soft and cool and easily tamed. The skin of his neck is warm and velvety. She can feel his pulse underneath her fingertips, thumping with adrenaline like a pinned animal paralysed with fear, waiting for the teeth of its predator. More than analogy, he has literally become her prey, lying willing below her and waiting for her attack. She imagines taking a blade and opening that vein, opening the artery beside it, kneeling by him as the blood pours out, tasting it, bathing in it, holding his face and watching his eyes as the consciousness drains out of him…

But, no. She takes a deep breath. No, that would not do at all. Even if a slave did consent, it would fail the sanity test. Just a dark fantasy, not something real. It is strange, though, how possessive she feels about this one. How violent. There's something special about him. He triggers some deep instinct in her. Did Richard know, when he bought him? Did he feel it too? Did he share this desire to take some kind of dreadful advantage over the poor creature? She shakes her head and tries to calm herself. No, best not to ask him. Richard would not be any deterrent. Richard would help her dispose of the body. And Sarah would do whatever he told her to. It would be Danny most likely to have a fit of remorse, weeks later, and call the authorities…

No. Damn, where is her mind wandering? Why is she even imaging such madness? Of course she won't betray Simon's trust. Stick to the agreed scene. Focus.

She concentrates on Simon's face. He remains silent.

He is innocently oblivious to her imaginings and somehow that makes him all the more attractive. She must be careful not to stray off the path. One false step and she may lose herself in the hunger.

"Are you comfortable?"

"Not really, Mistress. I feel like I'm about to fall flat onto my face."

Not exactly the reply she was expecting. Whatever happened to 'Yes, Mistress, and please would you hurt me now'? No wonder he positioned himself too far backwards. Oh well, at least ruining the mood will keep them on safer ground.

"Don't worry, you can't fall. It's bolted to the floor. You're not going anywhere."

He visibly relaxes, unclenching the tension in his back. At last, he releases his head down towards the floor.

"Good boy. Is that better?"

"Yes Mistress, much better. Thanks."

"Do you know why the bench is angled?"

"No Mistress."

"A slight inversion intensifies the feeling of being out of control. And it makes sure your backside is presented at the best angle for what's coming next." She lightly smacks his ass. He gasps – not from pain – so it must be from panic or else pleasure. Which?

He wriggles, or tries to, but he is trapped and utterly helpless. He makes a small moan. Pleasure, then. He is going to be vocal. Good – although that will really not help to keep the worst of her desires at bay. This is going to be fun.

"Colour?"

He takes a moment to remember how to respond.

"Green. Green, Mistress."

"Good. Shall we begin?"

"Yes please, Mistress." He is still eager. Her confidence increases that he will manage the pain ahead. She walks to the front of the bench and stands to the side of his head until he lifts it to look at her.

"What is your safe word?"

"'Stop', Mistress."

"Good boy. Then we are ready." She lifts the crop towards his face, so the tongue is in front of his mouth. He does not move. He does not know what is expected, silly boy, he is horribly unschooled. For a second she feels a flash of guilt before the hunger gushes back.

"You should kiss the crop, Simon. It is a sign of respect. You will kiss it now, and again after I have finished using it."

Simon nods, and stretches his face forwards to kiss the whip. His Adam's apple protrudes vulnerably from his extended throat. His eyes are wide with meek anticipation and he is beautiful. Just before she is about to prompt him, he whispers,

"Thank you, Mistress."

Alannah speaks quickly before her mind runs ahead of her.

"Good boy. I'm going to warm up your skin first. I will warn you before I begin the full strokes. Remember to keep breathing and relax as much as you can. Remember you have to go through the pain to come out the other side."

Moving to stand at the side of the bench, she places her left hand on the small of his back. At first, she rubs the tongue of the crop over Simon's buttocks, keeping full contact, sliding down over the top of his thighs and back, marking out the area she will work.

Gently, she begins bouncing the whip, moving from the wrist in a tap-tap-tap. Light, fast and even, left to right, up and down, she goes over each part of skin two or three times, spreading the movement across the whole area contained between the straps at his waist and his thighs.

He does not seem to be in any distress, and it would be strange if he was panicking so early, but she decides to be cautions and check in anyway.

"Colour?"

"Gree...een Mistress." He drags the vowel out in a languid sigh. He is enjoying himself. Irrationally, Alannah finds it irritating. There is something disrespectful in his enjoyment. He is obviously nowhere near an edge, and unsurprisingly so. Time to change gears.

"Good. Now we will begin properly. Keep breathing." She is determined have him begging for mercy before she lets him go. She will put an end to those lewd moans and make him really cry out for her.

She lifts the crop away from him, and swings it back down firmly across the middle of his ass. It sounds a satisfying small smack, and he makes an even more satisfying gasp.

She lifts the crop again. Swinging from the elbow she strikes again, leaving the faintest red line across the top of his legs. This time the noise he makes is a strangled sort of 'Mmh', with a rising inflection at the end that makes it sound plaintive.

She gives him a third touch, carefully placed away from the first two, before checking in again. Still green, and given with more trepidation now, which is pleasing.

Counting off the seconds between each stroke, she begins to build a rhythm. The trick is always in the timing. In keeping things slow and light for longer than you want to, and holding back from going too hard too soon. It's always tempting to ramp up too fast, especially with the noisy ones.

Carefully, with great self-control, she covers every inch of flesh with a gentle red glow before the sound has built up into the familiar satisfying thwack.

Nineteen

Taking It

Simon lets his head dangle as Mistress taps the crop over his ass. His weight rests on his legs and stomach as he hangs forward, pulsing dick crushed onto the bench underneath him. He moves his arms to test what motion the restraints will permit him – and finds he has only an inch in any direction before he meets the limit. His hands can grab the bench legs, but he cannot reach the floor, nor can he twist his fingers back far enough to unlock the clips securing his cuffs to the iron. The metal clinks together as he tries, as if laughing at his attempt. The sheepskin inside the cuffs presses firmly and insistently on his wrists.

He lifts and releases his shoulders, meaning to relax into the position, but the movement presses his waist against the thick strap and makes him feel all the more captive. There is no way to redistribute the weight from his knees, or shift the position of his legs. He can circle his ankles but that is all. She has him trapped.

The taps travel all over his buttocks and the backs of his thighs. They are gentle, and there is no pain yet. It feels erotic, being touched by her, even indirectly through the whip. He feels a tightening at the base of his cock, uncomfortable pressure but warm and welcome. Oh, this is good. This is what he wanted, this and everything else that has been promised.

Mistress speaks, and Simon's brain needs a second to understand the words. She is asking for a colour. Mistress wants to know if he is enjoying what she is doing. He wants to express himself, to craft words into phrases that could adequately convey his feelings, but he also wants to obey her rules.

"Green, Mistress."

Mistress says they are going to begin properly. Simon knows he has only received the introduction, and his stomach flips in fear at the thought of the coming pain. Too late, he is bound and helpless, and he is not even sure he wants to object. She swings the crop before he can think further.

The first strike lands, square across both cheeks of his ass. It shocks him, making him take a sudden breath. It hurts a little, but not as much as he expected. This is going to be OK.

The second strike lands lower, on his legs, where the thinner flesh is less able to disperse the energy of the blow. It still doesn't hurt much. It's not a nice feeling, but it isn't the unbearable sting he worried he might suffer. And being tied down, naked and in her service, that part is very nice indeed. He could get used to this.

The third strike is higher, and at an angle, slanting right to left. Mistress asks him for a colour again, and Simon answers quickly; "Green."

She continues. The next few strikes are much the same, and Simon begins to think this could be a disappointment. Is this it? Is she going too easy on him because he said he was nervous about the pain? Should he say something?

Then, slowly, the burning starts. Gently at first, a light tingling, a buzzing sensation around the place each stroke lands. An unpleasant tickling underneath his skin, like the crop is injecting a mild poison wherever it lands. This is not enjoyable any more. It is uncomfortable. Simon strains against the waist strap but it does no good.

"Colour?"

"Green, Mistress." He still wants to please her. It isn't bad, just odd. He will see where she takes him, for now.

"Are you beginning to feel it yet, Simon?"

"Yes, Mistress. It's kind of fizzing inside my skin."

"That's right Simon. Good boy. Things will begin to intensify from now on. Remember to keep breathing."

The strikes keep landing, each stronger than the last. The buzzing becomes painful. The shadow of poison left behind each blow no longer has time to fade before the next injection comes. His skin burns hotter as one impact stacks on top of the last, then another, and another, starting a crescendo of sharper and deeper pain until instinct takes over and he tries to fight it. He wriggles and wrestles but the straps hold him firm. He rattles his wrists against the bench legs, bucking his shoulders, but nothing works. Tight leather holds him in place so he is unable to avoid the pain, unable even to lessen it by changing the angle at which the blows land. She speeds up.

"Colour?"

"It hurts, Mistress. I don't like it. It hurts, and I can't move. Please."

"Colour, Simon."

The blows cease for a moment, and the respite is bliss, but at the same time he doesn't want her to stop. He doesn't want the pain but he doesn't want to be set free either. His dick is rock hard, and his ass is burning, and his knees ache, but more than anything else he wants this woman to be pleased with him. He wants to feel proud of himself.

"Orange, Mistress."

The whip starts again immediately. The pause from the pain makes it feel worse than before. Shit, that was a mistake. Should he have said red? Can he cope with this? Does he even want to?

"Good boy. You are doing very well, Simon, and that makes me happy. Keep breathing. Remember, first it's going to hurt, then it's going to feel different. You can do this. I want you to do this, for me. Keep breathing."

Her praise gives Simon a second's relief until the pain swells up into his mind again. Blow after blow rains onto his sore skin. It seems worse than before now, and it feels faster than ever. Simon bucks and tugs at his restraints, helpless. His distress is obvious. She must see it. She does not stop.

"Please, Mistress. Please, it hurts."

Once he opens his mouth the words fall out in a torrent.

"It really hurts, please. Just slow down for a while? Fuck, that hurts. Don't. Just don't, please. Please, Mistress. I want to rest for a minute. I don't like it. I don't want any more. I need to get up. Can you untie my legs, at least? Please? It hurts, everything fucking hurts. Shit, shit, shit. Oh God, let me go, it fucking hurts."

Even through the fog, he is aware of avoiding the one word that could end the pain. He sucks in air deeply, blowing it out, refusing to form it into the word 'stop'. Is it pride? Is it bloody mindedness? Lust? There is no thought outside the pain any more. He does not want it, but he will not stop it.

Mistress purrs, and concedes nothing.

"Keep breathing, Simon. You're doing fine. Keep concentrating on taking it well. You can do this. You can do it for me. Colour?"

"RED. Fucking red, you sadistic bitch." Simon spits his words out in frustration, pulling at his restraints, shaking in anger or in tears, or both. Every time he strains against the straps, he feels his dick compressed beneath him. Every blow she lands shudders its vibration between his legs, into his balls. It is worse than he imagined, and better, and he will do anything to make her stop except the one thing that will work. His instincts are screaming for escape, and yet, some secret inner part of his mind does not want this to end. It is ridiculous, and stupid, and it fucking hurts, and he hates himself for wanting it – but he does want it. He wants it badly. It makes no sense at all.

"Not red. Orange. Oh God, I think it's orange. It might be red. I don't know. Fuck, it hurts. I'm sorry, Mistress. I don't know. I don't know anything, Mistress, it just hurts. Please… it really fucking hurts. How long… how long are you going to… Please don't…"

Simon's voice trails away as his speech becomes less and less coherent. Mistress' voice is soothing but the words don't mean anything any more. They are just a noise. A smooth, calm noise that drifts past him. Everything feels far away now, further away every time the crop lands on him. It hurts, still, but it is different too. There is no point in fighting any more. There is nothing he can do to influence the events around him. He lies still, sinking under his own weight. The breath rushes inside him, and out, fast and light. The crop thuds again and again. His groin throbs, every part from his stomach down the inside of his legs, pulsing forwards into his swollen dick, somehow growing, growing still, ever harder. His mind is being pulled down, down into the heat under his skin, backward into the pain, forward into the pulsing shaft, down against the hot flat leather. All time has melted, become circular, measured in cycles of heart beats and whip beats and gasps of air.

*

After a long time, Simon understands the pattern has slowed. Things are coming back to him. He can feel his hands again. His breathing deepens. The air tastes cold.

Her hand, on his back. The crop has stopped.

His forehead is dripping in sweat. He is back inside

the room, part of the world again. The place in which his mind had taken refuge no longer exists. There is only reality now.

Mistress whispers softly to him.

"Good boy, Simon. Well done." She strokes his shoulder. "Very good boy."

She walks behind him, surprising him as her hand reaches between his thighs to release the straps. They fall away, one after the other. Inexplicably, Simon feels sad.

Sharp heat-pain, fading fast, as she lays a hand on his ass. Fuck, that hurts. Her other hand reaches underneath, near his dick but not near enough. It reaches under the table where he cannot feel her. A scrape of metal against metal, and the pressure on his waist lifts. He does not like it. It feels less safe.

Simon shifts his weight, peeling his stuck skin from the leather. His knee cracks. He is still hard, but he doesn't feel horny any more. He feels cold. He realises he is trembling.

"Good boy, Simon. Gently, now. Don't move too quickly. Keep breathing. Good boy."

Mistress walks forward, stopping next to his head. His wrists are still chained, but the rest of him feels more free than he thought possible. Hurt, but free.

Mistress lifts the tongue of the crop to his mouth.

"What do you say, Simon?"

Gently, he leans forward to kiss it.

"Thank you, Mistress."

Twenty

Aftercare

Alannah hangs the crop on the side of the cabinet, then grabs a blanket from the shelves before returning to the boy.

He did well. Very well, all things considered. Admittedly, he struggled at the start. He seemed close to using his safe word. But her instinct to push through had been justified. Once he was over the threshold he went in deep. He took it well, better than many with much more experience. He blossomed before her, the pristine virgin territory of his mind cracked wide open, splayed out under her. Pushed far beyond conscious thought, stripped of self-awareness, he remaining naked and unashamed until the last. It was wonderful to hold him under, to steep his body in pain until it turned mottled with the crimson, soaking it up, becoming ruined. What a privilege to place those first marks over a person's soul. He has potential, definitely. He will make a good little slave for someone. But not for her, sadly. He isn't a responsibility she wants. Lots of fun, but too much work. No, now she must put him back together before releasing him into the wild.

Alannah shakes out the blanket as she walks. He is still dazed. He lifts his head slowly at the sound of her approach, wide eyes blinking up at her. She smiles to reassure him.

"Good boy, Simon. You did very well. I'm going to take care of you now."

She drapes the blanket around him before stooping to unclip his wrists. He bends his elbows, flexing his fingers then making fists, re-establishing circulation. His breath is still a touch unsettled; he hasn't fully come down to land yet. She will be careful moving him, he could be dizzy.

"You can get down from the bench now, Simon. Don't move too fast, you will feel disoriented at first."

Simon props himself up on his elbows and lets out a shaky sigh. She moves closer, ready to catch him if he loses his balance. Gingerly, he reaches one foot towards the floor. He presses the ball of his foot down, then lowers his heel. The second foot follows. As he straightens to stand, the blanket slips off his hunched shoulders and falls to the floor. He tries to catch it, but he is not quick enough.

Alannah dips to the floor and retrieves it. Gently, she wraps the soft material around him once more, gathering the upper corners and twisting them around her hand.

"Can you walk yet?"

He nods, responding with a quiet, "Yes, Mistress."

"Good. Come and sit on the sofa for a while. I'll make you some tea." She leads him across the room by the corners of his blanket, providing stability for his faltering steps with the warm fleece. She indicates where he should sit, and he sinks down into the centre of the sofa. He pulls a pained expression as his weight transfers onto his ass.

"Owww. Damn, that hurts."

Alannah smiles wryly.

"Yes, I imagine it does. It will ease a bit soon. You're going to bruise up though. For now – tea will help."

The boy huddles into the blanket, looking like he might burst into tears at any moment. Sweet tea will bring his blood sugar back up, and that will help his mind to stabilise.

She busies herself with the kettle, filling two cups, stirring, dropping the teabags into the bin. By the time she returns to the sofa, Simon is looking even more gloomy. She sits next to him, handing one cup over.

"Here you go."

"Thank you, Mistress." He takes the cup, cradling it in both hands in front of his face. He keeps his eyes on the floor. Alannah watches him carefully for clues to his distress. Is it shame? Guilt? Self-hatred? This is a delicate point in their play, and her words must be well crafted. Alannah formulates her opening phrase, and is about to begin, when he speaks.

"Did I do it right, Mistress?"

She raises her eyebrows in surprise. He needs reassurance, then. But how softly he seeks it.

"Oh, sweet boy. Yes, you did it right. You did very well. I'm proud of you."

Tears well in his eyes. He tries to hide it, but the

wetness spreads down his cheeks. The trembling in his muscles gives way to shaking sobs.

"Damn. I'm sorry, I'm not normally like this."

"It's OK. It's just your brain chemistry trying to rebalance itself. There's nothing to be ashamed of."

He looks furtively at her through wet lashes.

"I just feel really…" his voice fades and he hangs his head, bringing the hot drink up to his mouth.

Alannah twists her body towards him, setting her tea down to one side.

"Poor thing. It's OK. Come here. I'll take care of you until you feel better." She spreads her arms to show him what to do.

Simon folds himself into her, leaning his head on her chest and curling his legs up behind him on the sofa. He is a warm, damp mess of blanket and tears and steamy tea. He seems very small now, like a child. Alannah wraps her arms around his head and strokes the hair out of his face.

"Ssssh. Hush now, Simon. Everything is OK. It will all seem better soon. You've been a very good boy. Ssssh, just rest now. Rest and let me take care of you."

She can feel him trembling beneath the blanket. She continues to soothe him, talking in a low voice, as he takes small sips of tea. Little by little, he stills.

After a while, the drink is gone and Simon lays calm on her chest. The shaking has subsided. The sugar has done its job. She can feel his eyelashes against her skin every time he blinks. Sweet boy. She kisses the top of his head, and he shifts his weight. She releases one arm, and picks up her cup again, draining it in two long gulps. He turns his face upwards, towards her.

"Thank you, Mistress." He looks less guilty now, and his shame has retracted to mere embarrassment.

"You're welcome, Simon. You earnt it."

He blushes a little, and his eyes crease into a smile.

"Did I, Mistress? I'm not sure if I did anything, really. Except lie there. And now, I feel a bit of a wreck."

"I've seen worse. You took the crop well. When the pain took you, you went down hard, and you've come in to land hard too. You're not used to it, yet. It will get easier the more you practise."

A light flickers behind his eyes when she said the word 'yet'. He adjusts his position again, with an awkwardness that could speak of the pain in his ass, or of throbbing in his cock. Time to move, before he gets any ideas.

"Excuse me, please."

She stands, taking his empty cup from his hand, and carries it with her own to the sink. By the time she returns he is sitting upright. She sets herself down on a chair, out of his reach.

"How is the pain, Simon?"

"I'm really sore, Mistress. But it's not as bad as before."

"Good. At least you'll have something to remember me by, every time you sit down for the next week."

He half-laughs and half-shrugs. The blood flares in his cheeks again, and a strand of hair falls forward over his shoulder. He is rather pretty, when he blushes. Perhaps that's why her hunger isn't quite sated.

"Is there any part of our play you want to talk about,

Simon? Any questions, or anything you want to tell me?"

"No, Mistress…" His intonation implies there is a question he is hesitant to ask. She tries again.

"Anything at all, Simon. It's best not to leave things unsaid. I promise I won't take offence. What is it?"

"Well… I wanted to ask… Was I good enough for you, Mistress?"

"Yes, Simon. I already told you, you did very well. You were a good boy."

"OK. Thank you, Mistress." He frowns. "It's just…"

Alannah sighs in frustration.

"It's just what, Simon? Spit it out."

"It doesn't feel like you enjoyed it, Mistress."

"Oh, that's sweet. Bless you. You don't need to worry about my enjoyment. I took exactly what I wanted. But it's rather lovely that you care."

He looks abashed. He falters over his words.

"I guess I don't understand what you like about it, Mistress. You don't… you don't want me to do anything else. Anything… sexual. Do you just like hurting people?"

Alannah lets the spike of anger pass before replying kindly.

"It's like that for some people. Richard is like that, sometimes. But not for me. I don't enjoy causing pain for pain's sake."

"Then… what, Mistress?"

"I like the feeling when someone yields to me. I like pushing a person outside their self control. I like looking into a person's soul, Simon, when they are barely a person any more. I like being the one holding the reins when they abandon themselves. That is what I wanted from you, Simon, and that is what you gave me. And it was beautiful. You were beautiful, Simon. I enjoyed you very much."

Silence falls between them whilst he contemplates her words. His eyes are full of adoration, but his mouth whispers only "Thank you, Mistress."

They sit in amicable peace for a time, until another thought occurs to him.

"Do you really have a violet wand, Mistress? Or was that just something you said to make me come home with you?"

She shakes her head and gives him a tight smile.

"Are you always this stubbon Simon?"

"I'm sorry, Mistress. I don't mean to be rude." He moves his legs, and winces in pain. It is... enticing. He appears unaware of the effect he is having. "I'm just trying to process everything that happened. Sorry if I shouldn't have asked."

"No, it's fine. I promised I wouldn't take offence. We do have a violet wand here. I would never lie to you, Simon. I can't abide lying. Honesty is one of the cornerstones of our house. Honesty, obedience and consent. But I don't think your brain chemistry can take another round right now, do you? I think it's best if the wand stays in its box for today."

"Yes, Mistress. I don't want any more pain. But... would it be OK just to look at it, please? I'd like to know how it works. If that's OK, Mistress?"

Alannah takes a deep breath, and holds it. Why does this boy have such good ideas, and such bad self-preservation instincts? She weighs the idea in her mind.

"Please, Mistress? I've never even seen one."

She exhales heavily, shaking her head. "Oh, for goodness sake boy. You're going to get yourself into trouble."

"I think I'd like that, Mistress."

Alannah walks towards the cabinet, her hunger surging once again.

Twenty-One

The Violet Wand

Mistress returns with a solid black box from the top of the cabinet. It looks like the kind of case that contains a musical instrument. A woodwind instrument, maybe, like a clarinet. A smooth, rectangular case with a beautiful secret inside. A secret which is not about the object itself, but about what you can create with it.

Shit, what is he doing? Asking for more after that… after the beating she gave him and the way it melted his mind. But it has twisted the need for her into his heart like a barb hooking the mouth of a fish.

He can't take any more pain. He feels fragile, bruised emotionally as well as physically. But he is not ready to go yet, either. Their play was drawing to an end, and he does not want to leave. He will do whatever it takes to stay near her, for as long as possible. Everything he dreamt of is real, and more. Now that he knows it, he does not care what she demands as long as she will let him stay inside this world she inhabits. The violet wand was a stupid idea, but it was all he could think of. And it worked. She returned with a box to show him, instead of asking him to leave. A black box with a forbidden secret inside. Simon's stomach turns over.

Mistress sets the box on the sofa between them. Two drawbolt latches hold it shut. Mistress reaches over and flicks each one open. They make a satisfying thud-dunk as they release. She cracks the lid. Inside, the case is lined with red velvet. Indentations hold a series of glass objects, each a different shape. To one side there is a shiny black tube, about nine inches long and made of plastic. It tapers at one end. Finger grips are moulded into the thicker end. An electrical wire runs out of it, looping in several figure-of-eights before terminating in a three pin plug. Inside a small well in the velvet lie smaller parts – a square pad, thinner wires, and several metal claws.

"There. One violet wand. Happy now?" Mistress does not sound angry. Simon doesn't want to provoke her, but he doesn't want the conversation to end either. What if she shuts the box and sends him home? Urgency, more than curiosity, persuades him to reach out a finger to stroke one of the glass bulbs.

"How does it work?"

She raises an eyebrow, and a shadow of some dark idea flashes across her face. Simon's body responds with a mixture of fear and arousal, a blend which already feels familiar. He revises his words before she points out his mistake.

"Sorry, I mean, how does it work please, Mistress? If I'm allowed to ask?"

She looks pleased. Is it because he corrected himself, or because he wants to know more? Or a different, unfathomed reason? Whatever the truth, she reaches into the box and lifts the black wand from its bed.

"This part," she gestures with the wand, "creates electrical stimulation. High voltage, low current. And this part," she picks up a round glass bulb with a glass stalk, "plugs into the wand and delivers the charge to the submissive. It is held near the skin, not on it, and it produces pretty little sparks as it is used."

Simon nods, as she returns the wand and bulb to their places inside the box. He looks with new understanding at the glass shapes. Rounded ends, thin wands, and rake patterns – different shapes for different sensations. His eyes rest on the metal claws. He reaches out and picks one up. It is made of brass and highly ornate. It looks like a prop from a fantasy film. He rolls it in his palm. A long point grows out of a ring shaped base. The tip is not sharp like he imagined, but slightly rounded.

"And these, Mistress? Do they work the same way?"

Her eyes glitter as she picks the object from his hand.

"No, Simon. These are for indirect play. The wand is used to electrify the dominant, and these are used to transfer the current to the recipient. Anything metal can be used... but these are rather beautiful, don't you think?"

"Yes, Mistress. I do. Does it hurt, Mistress?"

She nods.

"It can do. It depends how it's used, and who is using

it. It doesn't have to hurt much at all. The wide glass bulbs are the best place to start. These…" she places the ring on the tip of her index finger, and flexes it back and forth. "These are a little more specialised."

He smiles at her, and she smiles back. It feels like encouragement.

"Could we turn it on, please Mistress?"

She thinks about it, then shakes her head.

"It's a bad idea, Simon. You've had enough for one day."

"Please, Mistress?"

She shuts the box lid with a bang. Simon dare not move a muscle. She stares at the case, absentmindedly tapping the long brass claw on the edge. Gradually the tapping speeds up, then suddenly stops. She looks him straight in the eye, green fires burning into him. He smiles, but she does not return it, so he sheepishly drops his gaze downward.

"You are determined to court trouble, aren't you?"

*

Immediately, she is on her feet, dragging him across the room by the wrist cuffs he still wears. He struggles to avoid tripping as he jumps up and follows, caught in her wake. His legs feel stiff and his buttocks throb from the pressure of standing up suddenly. Friction glues the blanket to the sofa. It peels off his body as he speeds away, slipping behind and leaving him entirely naked. It isn't until they stop at the St Andrew's cross that he realises he is muttering panicked curses under his breath.

She spins him to face her, then slams his chest backwards so his body is thrown against the padded frame. The contact flares the agony in his ass again. In the moment it takes him to breathe through the pain and open his eyes, she has already clipped one cuff to the cross. He does not resist as she lifts his other arm and attaches it to the restraint.

She steps back, pausing.

"Do I need to tie your ankles too, or are you going to behave yourself?"

Simon is distinctly aware that he is naked, turned on, and it shows.

"I'll behave, Mistress."

"Good. You'd better. Now, spread your legs as wide as you can."

Moving his feet apart lowers his body, and stretches his arms flat against the cross. He sinks as low as he dares before his armpits complain about the uncomfortable angle.

"Do you have any metal inside your body? A pace maker, a joint replacement, anything like that?"

"No, Mistress. No piercings either, Mistress."

"I can see that, Simon." Her eyes slide over the likely places; ears, eyebrows, nose, lip, nipples, belly, then finally to his cock, turgid and exposed. As if noticing its state for the first time, she shakes her head and huffs disapproval.

"Do you have any heart problems? Any reason at all why applying an electric current to your skin is a bad idea?"

"Apart from the pain, Mistress?" He regrets the joke as soon as it is out of his mouth.

"If you give me that attitude, Simon, I will have to gag you. Don't think I'll hesitate."

"Sorry, Mistress. I shouldn't have said that. Please don't gag me. I haven't got any heart problems or anything like that, Mistress."

"Fine." She says it pointedly. Worry simmers up inside Simon's chest. He is tied up and alone with an angry woman in a room of torture equipment. Shit, why does he find it so exciting?

Mistress moves across the room to the cabinet. She takes out a pair of soft white slippers, the kind they provide in expensive hotels. She slips them on. Together with the silk robe, she looks like she is preparing to spend the afternoon in a spa rather than a dungeon. She reaches into the cabinet again and takes out a strip of leather with a red ball in the centre. A gag. Fuck.

She looks across at him.

"Just in case."

Mistress carries the black case from the sofa, setting it on the floor a few paces away. She lays the gag down next to it. The lid opens and she picks up the black wand, unfurling the lead until she reaches the plug. She gathers the cord into her left hand then reaches back into the box for a glass attachment. It is the round shape he touched earlier. It is not spherical but oval, a little flat on one side, with a long stalk protruding from the other. Carefully, she inserts the tube into the black wand.

She walks behind him, and Simon hears the familiar noise of a plug rattling into a socket. Mistress returns to him, closer now, close enough to touch him if she wanted to. She holds the wand up so he can see it, turning it one way then another.

"So?"

"So… Mistress?"

"So, ask me again, Simon. If you're sure you want to try it."

He smiles, realising what she means. He looks down at the bulb, just inches from his chest, and shudders.

"Could we turn it on, please Mistress?"

"Yes, Simon, I think we will."

Click – Mistress flicks the switch, and a low buzzing noise begins to hum. A purple-blue glow fills the glass, as sparks arc with a crackling rasp onto Simon's skin.

Twenty-Two

Both, or neither?

_____

Alannah holds the glass mushroom close to Simon's shoulder. The charge jumps from the wand to his skin in a thin web of purple. She lifts the glass away from him. The web narrows into one thicker band, and the snapping noise intensifies. He catches his breath.

"There. Do you feel it yet?

"Yes, Mistress. It kind of stings."

"Colour?"

"Green, Mistress."

"We are going to be very careful, Simon. Your capacity to cope with pain will be a lot lower now."

"Yes, Mistress."

He is full of trust, which is foolish but endearing. Returning to a second scene is against her better judgement. There is something about this slave that makes her want to push every limit.

She glides the mushroom upwards, following the line of his arm, staying away from the sensitive inner side and moving past his elbow. The hairs on his forearm stand on end, reaching towards the static of the glass and catching the purple arcs. He is taller than she is, and the slippers don't offer any extra height. She needs to stand close to the boy to comfortably reach up the length of his arm. She can feel his breath flowing past her ear, hear the tightness in his throat as he anticipates the pain. Smiling, she admits to herself she is standing closer than she needs to. She is teasing him with her presence. Like the wand, the trick is to maintain the correct distance. Too far and there is no spark, too close and contact diffuses the tension.

She dips her eyelashes and flicks her focus to watch his face. Her expression, soft at first, gradually hardens as she lifts her chin defiantly. With precision, using the edge of her peripheral vision, she pivots the wand from the outside to the inside of his arm. Purple sparks snap onto thinner skin, just beneath his wrist, where the nerve endings cluster. Does she just imagine it, or do the crackles sound louder?

His breath catches. She watches him trying not to flinch, forcing himself to leave his arm where she has placed it. He looks directly at her, something she would not normally allow, but today she finds it pleases her so she does not correct it. Instead, she studies the shape of his lips and the furrow between his brows. He looks back with glazed eyes which watch but do not fully see. His attention is stolen away from what his eyes take in by the sensation in his arm.

"It feels sharper on this side, doesn't it Simon? Where the skin is more delicate, and less used to being touched." He blinks, nodding. She floats the bulb downwards, past his elbow, lingering for a moment inside the fold before moving onwards to his armpit. The crease between his eyebrows deepens.

"Colour?"

"Green, Mistress." He stares longingly as he says it. She thinks how convenient it is to be able to place a subliminal suggestion with her eye colour. He is coping well with a return to pain. Time to change the pace of the game.

Taking a step back to a more appropriate distance, she lifts the wand from his skin until a strong single arc forms. She traces the contact point away from his splayed arms, downwards to his torso, seeking out his nipple. She notices his abdomen tense as the pain increases, relax as she traces across his chest, then tighten again as the arc reaches his other nipple. The movement makes his cock bounce. She stares at it, contemplating her next step.

The slave misinterprets her concentration as displeasure.

"I'm sorry, Mistress. I can't help it."

"That's OK, Simon. It's natural. It doesn't bother me. In fact…it could make things interesting. There are so many nerve endings in the penis, aren't there Simon?" She smiles as innocently as she can manage, and begins to snake the violet wand in a languid curve down his stomach.

The slave sucks in a deep breath in shock. He groans as the glass floats lower, lower still, until it is almost at his groin. At the last minute he takes a step and twists his hips away from the wand, away from the approaching torture.

She corrects his errant leg with a hard shove.

"You said you would behave. Don't move your feet."

"Sorry, Mistress."

"I don't want to stop and tie your ankles. If you make me, it will be so much worse for you. Put your foot back where it was."

He freezes, one leg on the floor and the other dangling stupidly in the air. Returning his foot will turn his abdomen back towards the wand. An inch or two further and the sparks will jump to the head of his cock. She can see him estimating the distance, trying to work out which part of his body the sting will reach. Will he obey and move towards the pain, or will he try to avoid it? She is not certain.

"Exactly where it was, Simon. I know you want to put your leg back so your feet are closer together than before. It might feel safer, but it is not. Having room to move your hips around won't help you at all. If you can't resist temptation and stay put, I will have to restrain you."

He looks suitably chastised. Gingerly, he returns his leg to its former position. She holds the wand as still as stone whilst he slips underneath it, back into his wide-spread pose. As he does, the purple tongue of electricity reconnects – first onto his hip, then rolling across his stomach, closer and closer to the centre. It slows as it nears his navel. His eyes fixate on the glass bulb. His breathing is fast and his forehead is damp, but he does as he is told, and manages to avoid shocking his cock in the process. She smiles. His obedience is pleasing.

"Good boy. That's better." She lifts the wand upwards, then slowly, ever so slowly brings it back down.

"Please, Mistress. Please don't move it any lower. Please don't put it on my dick, Mistress."

"Oh, Simon. How am I going to have fun if you keep setting new limits?" She draws small circles with the arc, moving from one side of his belly to the other, sliding ever lower.

"Please, Mistress. Please don't. It hurts bad enough where it is. Please don't do it."

"Colour?"

"Orange. Please Mistress. Orange. Please don't go any lower."

She sighs, feigning frustration.

"Oh dear Simon. Here I was thinking you *wanted* me to touch you. You're giving me very mixed signals you know?"

"Sorry Mistress. I'm not though. No mixed signals, Mistress. I'm turned on, but I don't want you to put that thing near my dick. Please, Mistress. Please don't put it there."

She tilts her head and lets the wand drift to one side, falling over the iliac crest and down the front of his leg. She waits until he relaxes a little before continuing towards his inner thigh, this time circling upwards towards his balls. He starts muttering obscenities under his breath, pleading for her to stop.

"Very mixed messages, Simon. On the one hand your voice is begging me not to touch you. And on the other, your body is throbbing for attention. I bet you're imagining it right now. Imagining how good it would feel to have a fist curled tight around your cock. A warm fist rubbing up and down, fast and firm, giving you all the attention you crave."

He whimpers. Of course, she can't go ahead and shock his genitals after such a clear withdrawal of consent. But she can threaten to do it. His erection looks painfully hard now, leaking fluid at the tip, straining upwards but finding nothing except cold air. He must be getting desperate.

"And orange... orange says 'persuade me'. Orange is not red. Orange wants to be green. Orange wants to be shown what it can do, if it only tries."

Keeping the wand dangerously close to his balls, she reaches out her left hand. As soft as a feather, she strokes one fingertip over the head of his cock. A long moan follows the finger's path, rising then falling as she takes it away.

"But you don't want me to touch you, do you Simon?"

"I do, Mistress." His voice is all gasps and whispers. "Please, Mistress, I do. I don't want that thing, but I want you. Please."

"Are you sure, Simon? There can't be any doubt. I'm not going to remove the wand. You may well receive a shock exactly where you fear. But I think you want to be persuaded, Simon. I think you want me to carry on. I think the fear is being drowned out by your body's need." This level of coercion feels uncomfortably strong, but the boy makes Alannah want to abandon common sense. Should she stop? It is certainly the safer thing to do. But no, it is not necessary. He has his safe word, if he needs it. Why shouldn't she enjoy him? She looks into his face, and asks the question.

"Do you want me to touch you, Simon?"

"YES. Yes. Oh, God, yes Mistress, please touch me. Please."

Bingo. Consent given. She can continue.

As if on cue, the wand's arc jumps from the slave's leg onto his ball sack. He yelps, shooting upwards as far as he can stretch, but he does not move his feet. Alannah rewards him by wrapping her left hand firmly round his shaft, squeezing tight without moving. The purple light flashes back into his thigh.

"Good boy."

The expression on his face is wonderful. He is full of longing and fear and all the base instincts. Desire wins, and he pushes his hips forwards trying to slide himself against her hand. His testicles come too close to the glass again, and a second painful shock makes him retreat. He calms himself, panting, his eyes pressed shut. A quiet groans escapes his mouth.

Patiently, she waits for him to learn the lesson. He swallows, then licks his lips. She maintains a firm pressure with her hand, and refuses to move it. Her other hand keeps the wand absolutely steady.

"Please, Mistress." He whispers it, in a low voice. "Please."

"Colour."

"Orange. Please, Mistress. Please. I want it so bad. Please do it, Mistress."

"I like orange, Simon."

He tries again to thrust forwards, at a different angle. He gets another shock to the balls, resulting in swearing and more panting as he forces himself to stay still.

"Please, Mistress. Please?"

"I like orange, and I like you Simon. So let's up the stakes. I'm going to give you a choice. Both or neither?"

The thinking part of his brain is not in control. He is sluggish to respond.

"What do you mean, Mistress? Please don't take your hand away. And please – I don't want you to hurt me any more."

"Well, that's up to you, Simon. We can end things here, if you like? We can put away the violet wand and finish our session. Or, we can keep going. I will even let you come. But only if you take some cock and ball torture whilst you're getting there."

She traces her thumb over his head, smearing the slick wetness over his glans, causing another long moan. He struggles not to push forward into her touch, knowing the pain that would result. She lifts the wand anyway, connecting underneath his balls and turning the moan into a shout.

"Your choice, Simon. You can have both..." she squeezes his shaft as he squirms to escape the burning spark.

Suddenly, she lets go, dropping the wand out of range and releasing his cock back to the cold air.

"...or neither."

Twenty-Three

A Happy Ending?

As soon as the wand is removed, the pain stops. Simon's relief is instant. The burning ceases and there is no lingering bruised feeling, unlike with the crop. For a moment he feels euphoric, until the throbbing in his dick begins to build. He is so horny, he just wants to rub himself against something. He misses the warmth of Mistress' hand on his flesh. He wants it back. No, not wants – it is beyond mere desire now – needs. He needs it back. Anything to feel some satisfaction from this overwhelming lust.

Simon breathes through it, forcing his mind to focus on something else, anything else. The stretch of his arms. The pressure on his feet. The soreness in his buttocks. Anything except the insistent urge that he wants her hand back regardless of the cost.

He recovers his mind a little. He licks his lips to moisten them whilst preparing to speak. He opens his eyes, but is too ashamed to look at her. Looking down is no better, all he can see is his own swollen dick, traitorously begging him to agree to her touch. He closes his eyes again.

"Please, Mistress. You've got me so turned on. I want it so bad. But please don't hurt me any more."

Mistress sighs. "Is that a no, Simon?"

"It's not a no, Mistress. It's a yes. I want it, please Mistress. Please touch me. It's just… I can't take any more pain."

"I understand, Simon, but my offer is clear. Both, or neither. No pain, no orgasm. It sounds like your choice is neither. Which is a real shame, because…" she steps up close to him, very close, pushing her body against his. The cool silk of her dressing gown brushes against his tip, followed by the glorious warm pressure of her body. Simon blinks his eyes open to find her face next to his. Her green eyes smile at him, her lips are close enough to kiss. She smiles, and continues, "…I thought you liked me."

Everything happens at once as Simon's stomach somersaults and he brings his lips towards hers, unconsciously crushing his groin onto her body, the beginnings of gratification tightening in his balls and realising with horror that he is going to cum far too quickly, just as soon as his lips reach that soft mouth… but suddenly she is gone. She steps away, laughing, leaving him hanging from his wrists in a sweet misery of need.

"Never mind, Simon." She walks to the black box and removes the glass bulb from the wand. "You're right, it's too much. Neither is the sensible choice. We had a lot of fun together, didn't we? Perhaps it's time to end." She opens the box, replaces the glass, then begins walking towards the plug, gathering up the cable. Simon's heart sinks. He squirms in frustration, humiliated, as he realises his desperate desire will overpower his common sense.

"Please…"

She pauses, the cable looped from palm to elbow, neither winding nor unwinding.

"Please, Mistress."

"What, Simon?"

"I want both." He hates himself for admitting it.

Mistress raises an eyebrow. "Are you sure, Simon? Haven't you had enough pain for one day?"

"Yes. I've had more than enough pain. But if it's both or neither then I want both. I need it. Please, Mistress." His cheeks redden with shame but his dick pulses eagerly. She turns towards him, dropping the cable to the floor.

"You really are beautiful like that, Simon."

He hates her and he loves her and all he can think of is persuading her to touch him so he can finally get what he craves.

"Thank you, Mistress. Please don't make it hurt too badly."

She smiles and shakes her head. "Don't worry, Simon. I won't be too cruel. And I can't imagine you'll suffer for long, given the state you're in."

He blushes again, but his self-loathing still burns less brightly than his desire.

She reaches into the box for the bulb, but pauses thoughtfully.

"The glass is fragile. I don't want it getting knocked and shattering. I have a better idea."

She reaches for the square pad in the velvet well. It is attached to a thin white wire, at the end of which is a small round plug. Mistress inserts the plug into the handle of the violet wand. She turns her back, loosens her robe, then slides the pad against the skin of her waist before tying the belt again. Delicately, she picks up four metal claws, sliding each one onto a finger.

"There," she announces, "Much less fragile. These are a better plan. Are you ready?"

Simon nods ruefully.

"Are you sure you want to do this?"

When Simon nods again, Mistress flicks the switch on the wand handle and the buzzing noise resumes, quieter than before. She prowls towards him.

One long brass claw carves through the air towards his chest. As it draws near, a spark jumps from the tip onto Simon's chest. He catches his breath. The sensation is sharp, like the glass bulb but more intense, searing into his skin until he smells burning. It hurts, and there is no fucking way he can take that on his dick. Shit.

Just as he is about to cry out, she slides the claw closer, until it touches his skin. On contact, the burning dampens to a painful buzzing sensation. He exhales heavily.

"How does that feel?"

"It really fucking hurts, Mistress. I think it's too much. Shit."

She smiles, curling her index finger and extending the middle one until the sparks jump from that point instead.

Lazily, she repeats the process with her ring finger and her little finger.

"Oh, that's a shame Simon. Is it really too much? You are changing your mind a lot today."

The sparks burn down Simon's torso, leaving behind a thin brown mark. He can't help yelping in pain.

She huffs, removing her hand and flicking the machine off again. Is it relief or disappointment he feels? She turns a dial on the handle then switches it back on. Anticipation floods back.

"Well, maybe we can turn it down just a little. I'm not trying to brand you today."

"Thank you, Mistress."

When the claws touch him again the pain is less intense. She wastes no time in lowering the contact point – downwards, over his stomach, straight down, onto the head of his dick. He screams.

Mistress' eyes widen but instead of pulling away she grabs hold of him, sending the buzzing fizzing sensation right through his shaft. He cries out again, part scream part moan. It hurts, but almost any feeling there is welcome after being hard for so long. He writhes against her touch, arching his back and flailing his arms as much as the restraints allow. She lets go.

"Colour?"

"Fuck. Holy fuck."

"That is not a colour, Simon."

"I know. Sorry, Mistress. It's just… I don't know. I can't think. Fuck."

"Have you changed your mind? Would you prefer

to have neither? You only need to say 'stop' if you've had enough."

"No. Shit, sorry Mistress. Orange. Please bring your hand back. It hurts but I want to keep going, please Mistress."

She smiles a terrifying half smile.

"Good boy, Simon."

Once more, she slides the claws across the skin of his cock, slowly, excruciatingly, until he lets go of whatever inhibitions remain and screams at the top of his lungs. She grasps his shaft again, lessening the pain, increasing the pleasure, increasing his desperation to reach orgasm. He is breathing hard by the time she lets go, hoping for another few seconds of respite before he submits himself once more. She does not grant it.

Instead, he gets worse pain, much worse, this time underneath his balls, burrowing inside him like lava erupting between his legs into the soft flesh. He tries to escape it, backing up against the cross until the bruises on his ass complain too. The agony is too intense for him to breathe, he can't even mutter his safe word. When she finally stops he is gasping, sweat running down his face, and worse still, losing his erection.

The bitch is still smiling at him.

"Well done, Simon. Very well done. Good boy."

"Fuck you." He spits as much fury into the words as he can muster.

She giggles. "Well, yes, that's the general idea."

"Fuck you. Let me go."

"Sssssh, now. Poor Simon. Keep breathing. If you really

want me to let you go, you need to use your safe word."

He remains silent, tight lipped.

"That's what I thought."

She gloats, triumphant, but switches off the wand before bringing the claws back to touch him. This time she is gentle, massaging the brass along his length until he stiffens again and begins to buck into her rhythm. Just when his enjoyment grows, she lets go.

"Ssssh, there's a good boy."

"Please. Please keep going, Mistress."

The machine hums back to life. The claws advance again, fizzing then burning then more fizzing, never quite bearable. They crawl their pain over him, sparks jumping from one brass tip to another whilst he endures and waits for it to stop. Stop, or change at least. To morph in quality and bestow on him a greater portion of pleasure amidst the agony. Still it goes on, sharp fire dancing into him, until finally he can't take any more.

Yelling curses, he writhes and twists, banging his arms against the cross – but cannot escape. Then he remembers his feet. His feet are not tied. He can move his legs. He can get away from this burning. Without thought for his disobedience, Simon brings his feet together and rises up on tip toes. Instinct brings one knee high across his body in protection, deflecting the fire away from his suffering dick.

Blessed relief, but only for a second.

With a violence belying her calm expression, Mistress slams his leg out from under him, leaving him dangling from his arm restraints. Reflexes try to arrest his fall by stamping his feet back down on the floor. She presses her advantage, stepping a slipper over one foot to hold it down as she brings the brass claws back up to his genitals.

This time it is even worse. His foot hurts and his ass hurts but most present of all is the inferno at his dick – inside, underneath – burning and burning as her hand twists and rubs. She has him pinned. Fuck. How did he end up here? Why did he agree to it? How did she persuade him to take more pain than he knew existed? And why does some part of him still enjoy it? Still need it, even beg for it?

Despite the pain, or perhaps because of it, Simon's excitement increases. The throbbing coalesces, becomes something more. It starts to build. The primal noises spilling from of his mouth become throatier, transitioning from yelps into moans. Euphoria begins to dampen the pain, and Simon begins to ride the rhythm. It hurts, but it is good. It is all consuming, ripping through him and taking over every corner of his mind. He is close, very close to orgasm. This time he remembers to ask permission.

Shakily, he cries, "Mistress, please may I come?"

She slows the rhythm a little. "Are you sure you want to? It's so messy. You'd have to clean up."

"Yes! Please Mistress? I'll clean up. Please. Oh God, please let me come Mistress, I'm so close."

"Well… Since you asked so nicely…" she grinds her foot on top of his, "…no."

She lets go of his cock, removing the sparks but leaving him burning anyway.

"Oh God, no Mistress, please no, I need it. I need more."

"No, Simon. I think I'll grant your first request instead."

"My first what? I don't know what you mean, Mistress. Please, Mistress. I need it. PLEASE."

"Your first request, Simon. A few minutes ago. To let you go."

"No, no no no. Please don't, Mistress. I'm sorry. I didn't mean it. I need more. Please give me it, Mistress. Please let me come."

His words fall on deaf ears. She flicks the switch to turn the violet wand off. Simon panics, rabid with need, begging and pleading as she reaches up and unhooks his right cuff from the frame. Her foot screws down on top of his as she leans upwards. Mistress gently bends then lowers his reluctant arm, which is stiff from immobility. He knows better than to try touching her. He can only repeat his apology and beg her to change her mind.

She cuts him off. "Ssssh, Simon. That's enough."

Disappointment leaves him inconsolable. Nothing is left except strong emotion and unmet desire. He stops begging but can't supress the whimpers of frustration.

She looks at him condescendingly. "Silly boy. I said both, and you shall have both."

His shame tinges with confusion.

"But I shan't be getting messy." She takes hold of his loose hand, bringing it up to her face. She turns it over, and licks a long wet trail across his palm and down his thumb. Moving his arm downwards, she presses his slick hand onto his cock.

"I'm sure you can manage this part on your own. Remember, you will NOT move your feet."

Simon realises what she means, grasping hold of himself and beginning the familiar motion up and down. She nods, and fiddles with the dial on the wand. Oh God, did she turn it down or up? Simon shudders and moves his hand faster.

"This will sting a bit, Simon. I'll stop when you stop, understood?"

"Thank you Mistress." Simon can barely get the words out as she flicks the switch and he pumps furiously, racing against the coming pain, revelling in being allowed satisfaction at last.

"Good boy. You may come whenever you want."

She places her claws under his balls and the pain sears through at exactly the same moment Simon ejaculates. He screams, loud and open throated, pain and pleasure perfectly overlapping in tortured ecstasy.

Mistress steps expertly aside, avoiding the fluid which splatters down to the floor. She flicks off the wand. One final drip runs down Simon's leg as his dick softens. Mistress runs a clawed finger up his thigh, scooping up the thin liquid. She smiles.

"Good boy, Simon. Now that really is the end of our playtime. You've been a very good boy, but a very messy one too. Time to clean up. Open."

She slides the metal into Simon's mouth.

Trembling, he is too weak to protest. Mildly disgusted, he sucks his own semen off her claw.

Twenty-Four

Lick

———————————

Alannah carefully removes the brass rings from her fingers. Flexing the stiff joints, she reaches the hand into her dressing gown and peels the contact pad from its position against her waist. The square is warm from her body heat. She absent-mindedly rubs the metal with her thumb as she unplugs the fitting from the violet wand and stoops to replace the tool in its box. She takes out the used glass bulb, gathering it together with the other items to be cleaned. Drifting across to the sink, she places them in the basket. Sarah will see to them later.

She glances up towards the window. The afternoon light is already fading – it must be later than she thought. How long have they spent in this dungeon? How long did she take brushing his hair in the bedroom? Still, there is no reason to hurry. There are no clients until tomorrow, and the paperwork for the club can wait a few days. Why not enjoy herself whilst she has the opportunity? She rolls her shoulders, clicking her bones, and sighs. Perhaps there is one more use for this boy before she dismisses him.

She walks back towards him. He is quiet now, waiting patiently for her instruction. One wrist is still restrained above his head, the other hangs by his side. Pleased, she notes he has not moved his feet.

"Good boy, Simon."

He lifts his face to smile at her, melting whatever embarrassment remains after his noisy abandonment.

"Thank you, Mistress."

She reaches up and unhooks his left cuff from the frame. Drawing both his wrists together, she begins to unbuckle the leather.

"You may move your feet now, Simon."

He shuffles his legs together, growing taller but somehow meeker too. A small strand of hair, not quite long enough to be held by the band, falls forward over his face. Golden, like the light at this time of day. He really does look beautiful, this newly broken thing. The hunger flickers again, surprising her in its persistent insatiability. Is it the boy, or a sign of her changing appetites? Either way, it does not matter. She wants him and she can have him. Yes, why not use him one more time before releasing him back to return to wherever he came from.

Removing the restraints, she gently rubs the indentations marks on his skin. They will disappear in an hour or so. No parts rubbed raw, no tears or breaks in the skin. These are good cuffs, worth the price for the quality.

"Time to clean up now, Simon." She glances to the

semen spattered floor to make sure he understands.

He nods, then quietly asks, "Where can I find the tissues, Mistress?"

"You won't need them, Simon."

He frowns. "Then how can I clean up, Mistress?"

She rolls her eyes. Stupid boy. "The same way you cleaned the claw, Simon. With your mouth."

He pulls a face and raises the back of his hand to his mouth in a wave of nausea. "Please, no Mistress. Not off the floor."

She shakes her head. "You've been such a good boy, Simon. Taking the wand so nicely after taking the crop too. Don't spoil it now."

"Please, Mistress. I don't want to."

"I told you that you would have to clean up. No excuses, Simon. On your knees and clean up your mess. NOW."

Simon lowers himself onto all fours and slowly crawls towards the first wet patch. Alannah stands over him. Leaning down, she gently tucks his loose strand of hair behind his ear. She doesn't want that lovely hair getting wet. Not after she went to so much trouble to clean it and dry it.

The slave looks at the blob of liquid in disgust. Licking up his mess will do him good. It will help him to learn obedience. Teach him to be more grateful for being allowed to ejaculate in the first place. But the poor puppy looks green at the thought. Alannah is not sure she can be bothered to summon the effort to discipline him.

He brings his face towards the ground and extends

his tongue. He dips it into the gelatinous pool, and immediately recoils, screwing up his nose.

"Oh, come on now, Simon. At this rate you will be here all night. Get on with it."

He looks up at her, pathetically, but she does not concede. He must understand his place, he must learn who is in charge. For his own good, but also so she can be sure her next plan is safe. She encourages him again.

"It came out of your body. It can go back into your body. It's not going to kill you. You don't have to like it, but you do have to clean it up."

He nods, and whispers, "Yes, Mistress." With a look of revulsion, he squeezes his eyes tight shut and quickly laps up the whole mess. He clamps his mouth shut and shudders. He tries to swallow but begins to retch. She watches him trying to contain it, forcing himself to push it down, holding back the urge to vomit. Eventually he conquers himself, and swallows.

"Good boy." She takes a step away and points out the next smear. "Now here."

The slave looks paler than ever as he shuffles forwards. His stomach heaves before he has even lowered his head to lick the floor. He pauses for a few breaths, then brings his tongue to the floor. He retches again, this time making the tell-tale sound of someone about to lose the contents of their stomach. He tries again to obey, reluctantly opening his mouth towards the stone, but he cannot bring himself to dip his tongue to the wetness. Alannah decides she has made her point. She does not want vomit on the dungeon floor as well as semen.

"Stop. That's enough. There are tissues under the sink. Go and get them quickly before I change my mind."

He practically runs to the sink in relief. He scrubs the remaining three wet patches of floor until they are dry, then sits back on his heels.

"Thank you, Mistress."

"Hmmm. Well, I don't want you throwing up in my dungeon, Simon. You tried your best. You failed."

"I'm sorry, Mistress. I just couldn't do it. It was horrible."

"Do you still feel sick?"

"Yes, Mistress, a bit."

"Well, in a moment you can put those tissues in the bin and rinse your mouth out in the sink."

"Thank you, Mistress."

"And then, you are going to wash your hands with warm water and soap. You need some time to level out after our last scene, and I would like to relax. You've been a very good boy, even if you weren't quite up to this last task. You tried to be obedient. So, I'm going to allow you a treat."

"A treat, Mistress?" He looks sceptical, but hopeful.

"I'm going to let you touch me."

His eyes go wide and he nods enthusiastically. "Yes, please Mistress."

"No, Simon, not like that. Nothing sexual. I don't want an orgasm from you, and you're certainly not going to fuck me. I doubt you'd be able to even if I allowed it. Not after your balls just got fried on my wand."

He hides the disappointment as well as can be expected.

"I didn't mean that, Mistress. I wouldn't... I know better now. I meant 'yes' like... like anything you want Mistress. I'll do whatever you want." He looks so pretty when he's humiliated. It really isn't fair to tease him further, which is exactly why she is going to enjoy it so much.

"I'm going to allow you to massage me, Simon. If you can be trusted, that is?" She pauses, making it a question.

"Yes, Mistress. I can be trusted, Mistress. I promise."

"I'm glad to hear it, Simon. Because if you can be trusted, I'm going to permit you to put your hands on my back and ease the tension out of my shoulders. I hope you have warm hands, Simon, and I hope you know how to get knots out of muscles. You can't imagine how stressful it is arranging those events, Simon. I'm very tense, and you're the closest thing I've got to entertainment right now. Do you think you can make yourself useful?"

"Yes, Mistress. I can be useful."

"Good boy. Now go and rinse that mess out of your mouth. Make sure your hands are clean. Clean, and warm, Simon."

"Yes, Mistress." He scurries off to the sink, soggy tissues in hand, eager to please.

Alannah smiles to herself, and saunters over to the cabinet in search of oil.

Twenty-Five

Oiled

———————————

Simon sloshes the water around his mouth and spits. He can still feel the salty goo, clinging to the back of his throat. He cringes to think of what he did. Disgusting. But however degrading the act, the fact that she made him do it still makes his soul sing. To be tortured into the most violent climax of his life, then forced to do that. It makes him feel dirty, but he loves the feeling of being used. Used however she wants.

And now he gets to put his hands on her.

He knows he won't be able to get hard again for a while. His face burns from the fact she pointed it out. It's as if she can see right inside his head, see exactly where his vulnerabilities and desires lie. And now she's going to let him touch her. Now, whilst he's impotent, mentally and physically. She made him that way. He wasn't lying when he said he will do whatever she wants.

He rinses his mouth a second time, gargling the water, willing it to dislodge the stickiness in his throat. Spitting, he swivels the tap from cold to hot, and reaches for a pump of soap. Clean, she said. Clean and warm. Oh God, he's going to get to touch her.

When he turns around, Mistress is lying on the sofa, facing away from him. She lies on her stomach, elbows wide and hands underneath her chin. She is partially undressed, so that her back and legs are exposed. Her skin looks smooth and taut, and enticingly warm. Her robe covers only the curve from her lower back to her thighs. The silk hangs loose, spilling off the couch down to the floor, promising that it might easily fall, leaving her naked. Simon allows himself to stare, enjoying the thought that she might let the cloth slip, might let him do more than just massage her. He savours the idea, despite knowing it is futile self-deception. That much is confirmed as he notices the far side of her robe is firmly tucked underneath her hips. A deliberate illusion, then, meant to tease him. It doesn't matter. At least she cares enough to torment him. She wants him for something, and whilst she does, he will provide as much or as little as she allows.

A sense of longing deepens within his core, purer than a sexual desire, a growing need to be wanted, appreciated, praised. A need for Mistress' approval. Satisfying that urge is becoming more addictive than simply chasing an orgasm, or any other physical pleasure. Simon starts to comprehend how this lifestyle could swallow him up, could take over his world and become his singular focus. What more is there to desire, besides Mistress' pleasure?

What more to attain, besides her satisfaction?

He walks towards the sofa stopping at a respectful distance besides her. She does not move a muscle. Perhaps she has not heard him approaching. Perhaps she is just playing mind games with him. He decides to break the ice.

"I'm ready, Mistress. My hands are clean and warm."

Mistress lets out a lethargic sigh.

"Mmmmh, in that case you'll need this…" She stretches one hand to the floor and picks up a dark blue glass bottle, waving it vaguely in Simon's direction.

He takes the bottle from her hand. His fingers briefly brush against hers; a jolt of excitement shoots up into his arm and across his chest. God, he's going to get to touch her.

Not knowing what to do next, he stands and waits in awkward silence until she turns her head to look at him.

"Come here then. You're not much use to me over there."

"Shall I kneel down, Mistress?"

"Certainly not. You won't manage an even pressure from the side. No, come and sit here." She tilts her head and pats her ass provocatively.

Oh fuck, she wants him to sit on her. Is it true, or has he misinterpreted? He is completely naked. Does she really want him to sit on top of her, with only a thin layer of silk between her body and his? For a moment the room seems to spin. He takes a step to steady himself, but finds his feet moving forward of their own volition. In slow motion they glide one, two steps. Unbidden, his left leg sweeps upwards, floats over her back, and plants itself down on her far side. Gingerly, he lowers his weight towards the sofa until he is straddling her. He freezes, waiting to hear if he has done the right thing or if he will be punished. The warm silk radiates heat from the back of her thighs to the inside of his. It feels glorious, a gentle balm soothing the place between his legs where the pleasure-pain had robbed him of his dignity. He holds his breath and basks in the glow, fearful that any moment now she might castigate him for his insolence.

Mistress breaks the spell with another sigh.

"Make sure you warm the oil in your hand first, Simon. And don't use too much."

"Yes, Mistress." He manages to whisper it without his voice shaking. He unscrews the black cap from the bottle and pours a pool of oil into the palm of his hand. Carefully, he replaces the cap and sets the bottle on the sofa besides him. Dripping as little as he can, he rubs the oil between his hands until it reaches body temperature.

"Mistress, may I begin?"

"Yes, Simon, you may. I like a firm pressure. My right shoulder needs the most work. I'll tell you when to stop."

"Thank you, Mistress."

Gratefully, he places his hands flat on the middle of her back, sweeping upwards to her neck, out to the sides then down towards her ass, spreading the oil across her skin. He repeats the motion two more times to make sure the lubricant is well distributed. When it is, he slows his hands, pressing his thumbs between each vertebra, rocking gently upwards one bone at a time. He digs his fingertips into the muscles of her shoulders, circling deep into the tissue until he reaches her neck. Finally, he brings his hands outwards and sweeps them down the outer edges of her back with a solid pressure, down to the base of her spine to start over again.

He continues the pattern, slick flesh melting under his hands. Her body seems to radiate with life, sending small vibrations travelling up his fingers into his wrists and up his arms. The oil smells of orange blossom, a scent to stimulate and invigorate, not masculine but not entirely feminine either. The tingles play on Simon's hands like sunlight.

He concentrates, feeling honoured that she allows him this intimacy, careful not to make any mistake which might bring this to a premature end. He attends to each shoulder in turn, pushing at the tight knots, worrying at them until they melt under his thumbs. Mistress sighs and shows her pleasure with deep rumbling purrs. Time begins to change its nature, slowing and parting around them like a river flowing around a rock, no longer touching them. She lies absolutely still beneath him as his hands stroke up and down the length of her body. She is warm and relaxed and so beautiful. Soon enough his veneration turns to yearning, and he feels the familiar swelling between his legs.

He tries to stay focussed on his work, ignoring his firming erection, trying to think only of Mistress' instructions. It is useless to do anything else. She has made it clear she won't have sex with him, no matter how much he wants to. No matter how much heat he can feel smouldering under his balls, rising from her body into him, warming the blood pumping through his dick.

Mistress shifts her weight, a tantalising rock of her hips underneath him. He tries not to moan. Luckily, the sound is hidden by a crack of her back. She stretches the joint out, then settles again.

"Mmmh, that's better. Good boy, Simon. Don't stop yet. Go back to those long deep movements you started with."

God, why did she have to use those words? The images in his mind… The bittersweet ache for more than he can hope to receive. She is toying with him, of course. Everything she does is deliberate. Still, here she is, lying bare-skinned underneath him, granting permission for his hands to run across her body, telling him she doesn't want him to stop.

Concentrate. Dammit, concentrate. Stop imagining what you can't have. Focus on what you're doing.

He tries to limit his thoughts to her muscles, to applying a firm pressure all the way up her spine then all the way down her sides and back to her tail bone. He tries, but every time he brings his hands together at her lower back he can't help but brush his wrists against his dick. Every time he slides his thumbs up her spine he can't help feeling the curve of her waist flowing beneath his fingers, wordlessly reminding him that she is a woman, a beautiful naked woman, lying underneath him.

He is so fixated on supressing his craving that when it happens he jumps out of his skin.

A knock on the door. Sudden, loud, insistent.

Mistress groans and lifts her head.

"What is it?"

"May I come in?" A man's voice. Is it Danny, Master Richard or someone else?

*

"Yes, come in."

Shit. Simon moves his hands to his lap in panic, trying to hide his obvious arousal. He does not want any man to walk in on him naked and hard, especially not...

Master Richard.

Simon's first thought is the threat he made to help Mistress to break him in. Then, with horror, he realises he has been discovered stark naked and straddling this man's undressed wife. Any other man would let fists fly first and ask questions later. Simon fears that Master Richard will be much more calculating about making him pay.

Richard smiles at Alannah.

"I'm sorry to interrupt. Having fun?" There is no hint of aggression, no jealous rage. Simon is confused.

"Mmh, yes," she replies, lazily, "What's wrong? Does Sarah need the hospital?"

"Oh no, she's fine. A bit swollen, but nothing I can't deal with at home. She's going to bruise up beautifully." He pulls a lewd smirk.

"Then what is it?" Mistress props herself up on her elbows, pushing Simon's weight backwards as she lifts her shoulders, exposing her chest to the Master's view. She seems to have no embarrassment at being found like this, no fear that her husband might object to the situation. If you can call that monster a husband. Simon's skin crawls at the thought. How can she be married to that? How can she allow herself to be seen, touched – and God, what else? – by this deviant terror of a man? To allow his eyes to slide up and down her body? If it is possible to mentally undress someone who is already naked, Richard is doing exactly that. Simon glowers with fear and hatred.

"Do you realise what time it is?"

"No, why? Is it late?"

"Dinner is almost ready. Shall I tell Danny to lay a fifth place?"

"Oh goodness, really? I completely lost track of time." She rises from the sofa, pushing Simon off her until they are both standing up. She makes no attempt to cover herself. Spinning around, she orders him to stay.

Even the fear of Master Richard can't tear Simon's eyes from her breasts. He watches, open mouthed, as she retrieves her robe and wraps it around herself. She turns her back on him, bends over to retrieve the oil, then walks across the room to the cabinet.

Suddenly he feels warm breath by his ear, and a pressure dragging down on his ponytail, preventing him from escaping. Shit. Master Richard has hold of him, his mouth close against his ear. How did he cross the room so fast? Mistress has her back to them and is too far away to intercede.

"I see you, looking at her. I know you want her." Richard begins, his voice accusatory. Shit. Oh shit, he's going to kill me. Or worse.

"I could tell you what it feels like. To fuck her. To hold

her in your arms and push deep inside that delicious cunt until she moans for more."

Master Richard's body presses up behind him. Simon squirms, but can't get away. His hair is held firm. What the hell is he doing? What is the safest thing to say? Oh Christ, when will she turn around and rescue him?

"But it would be pointless. You will never experience it. She will never, ever let you fuck her. Not because she holds to any antiquated idea about marital monogamy. Because she doesn't want you. Because she will never let a common slave like you defile her. It's a kindness that she allows you to serve her at all. You will never be good enough for her."

Simon's face is burns with shame as he feels the truth of the words. His eyes begin to well up. Hopelessly, he tries to swallow down the tumbling feelings of inadequacy, terror, longing, despair.

Finally, Mistress turns. She sees them, and inclines her head.

"Richard…? Put him down. Mine."

"Oh, we're just having a little chat, aren't we slave? You've had him all day. When do I get a turn?"

Please, no. Simon stares at her imploringly, willing her to make him stop. He cups his hands firmly in front of his withering dick and clenches his buttocks together.

"You've got your own one upstairs."

"Yes, but he's busy cooking. I want to play with this one." Master Richard lets go of his ponytail and runs a finger down the length of his back. Simon shudders in revulsion. "He's so… fragile."

"Oh, Richard, stop it. Look at him, he's terrified. What on earth did you say to him?"

"Just a little man-to-man talk."

She raises an eyebrow and waits.

"We were talking about how he'll never be allowed to fuck you, no matter how desperately he wants to."

She laughs. Another deep wave of shame crashes over Simon, swallowing up any sense of thankfulness that Mistress has not yet handed him over to her husband.

"Oh dear. What's got into you? You're not normally like this. You're not… jealous?"

Master laughs heartily. "Of this?"

Simon feels a sharp smack on his ass, before the Master walks towards Mistress.

"Don't insult me. No, I'm just feeling particularly proud of you recently. And perhaps a little protective." He wraps her into an embrace.

Mistress slides her arms around the devil's waist, smiling happily. "Good. For a moment I was worried you'd want to fuck me in front of him just to salve your masculine ego."

Richard brings his face close to hers and plants a tender kiss on her mouth, before looking back over his shoulder towards Simon.

"You know, I might enjoy that. But dinner is almost ready. Nothing worse than lukewarm food."

He untangles himself from her arms, and strides back towards the door.

"I'll give you some space to clean him up and get rid of him. Unless you want Danny to set a fifth place?"

"Oh no, it's family time. It wouldn't feel right."

"I don't mind. It's amusing having him around. He's so flighty, just one tiny push and he's a wreck. I like that in a man. Like a younger version of Danny."

"Well now, there's another good reason to send him home. Remind me, what are your house rules my love? Honest, obedience and…?"

"Goddamn bastard consent. Shame." Master Richard shakes his head, takes one last look at Simon, then walks out.

Mistress giggles, calling out after him. "I'll be there in five."

Turning to Simon, she asks softly, "Did he scare you?"

Simon shakes his head, blinking the wetness from his eyes. He is relieved that Master Richard has gone, but the price he took is high. His time with Mistress is over.

"A little, Mistress. It's OK as long as you're here. I know you won't let him hurt me."

The words seem to please her, and she smiles kindly.

"Good boy, Simon. You've been a very good boy all day. Come on, you can wait for the car upstairs. I'll have Sarah bring your clothes."

With that, she glides out of the door.

Simon picks up the towel from the floor, wipes his oily hands, and wraps it around his waist. He follows her up the stairs, back into the real world.

Twenty-Six

Goodbye

Alannah ascends into the delicious smell of Danny's cooking. Roast beef, or maybe one of his pies. Definitely something full of red meat. She inhales deeply, her stomach springing alive with hunger, so strong it is tinged with nausea. She could eat a horse.

The slave appears behind her. He is no longer naked. He has found a towel to cover his modestly. Richard did go a little too far with him. The dynamic in their relationship is changing, morphing and growing into something else. Something even better, she hopes. Protective, that's what he said. From anyone else, that would feel patronising and make her angry. From Richard, it makes her glow. She realises that she has completely forgiven him for last week's argument.

Still, although his stunt was funny, it was hardly fair on the poor boy. The slave is more than a little scared, regardless of what he claims. Poor lamb, and after he did so well too. Best to get him packed up and safely on his way before Richard gets any more ideas. She really hates to reign in her husband's appetites – it's much more fun to stoke the fires and watch the world burn – but only when it can be done responsibly, with willing victims. Not like this one. Why frustrate the one and upset the other?

Alannah turns and smiles at Simon.

"Come on, let's get you sorted out and safely on your way home."

The boy steps out of the stairwell, and Alannah clicks the dungeon door closed behind him.

"You can wait through here until the car comes."

She steps across the hallway into the dining room. Surprisingly, it is Sarah and not Danny who is laying the table; four places of gleaming silverware and glasses. Something must have gone wrong in the kitchen. Hopefully nothing that threatens the food.

Sarah has laid the side plates on the wrong side of the settings. The girl has been told many times, but she seems to have reached adulthood devoid of any sense of left or right. Alannah considers whether to intervene to correct the error, or leave it to Richard? She decides to leave it. His slave his problem. She has her own to deal with.

She pulls a chair out from the table, at the opposite end to the place settings, near the large sash window. He won't be in the way here.

"Sit."

He slides silently onto the chair, crossing his arms nervously in front of him.

She circles around the whole of the table to avoid squeezing between him and the wall. Sarah is putting out the glasses and appears almost finished.

"Sarah, did your Master give you more instructions for after you finish laying the table?"

"No, Mistress." She shakes her head, frowning. She often does, but Alannah has come to ignore it. She is not the kind of slave to be surly in quiet rebellion against obedience, the opposite in fact. Sarah tries so hard to please that her concentration makes her appear grumpy. It took a while to get used to it when she first moved into Richard's house. Now she recognises it for the positive sign it is. Not that Sarah's mood should affect her at all. It would be exhausting living with slaves if you let their emotional state rule your own.

"Then would you please fetch Simon's clothes? And his bag – it's in my room."

"Yes, Mistress." She shuffles off, still blissfully unaware of her mistake with the plates.

Alannah takes out her phone and calls Elvis. As reliable as ever, he answers immediately. She asks him to bring the car as soon as he can, and informs him that he is to return the slave home. Somewhere in Zone 3, Simon had said. She can't recall if he mentioned exactly where, but it doesn't matter, Elvis will work it out and she isn't particularly interested.

"Ten minutes, Simon. My driver will take you home. You need to be ready when he arrives, he can't park on the main road for long."

"Yes, Mistress." Simon looks more sullen than Sarah

did. He hugs his arms tighter across his belly, and fiddles with a corner of the towel.

"Will I see you again, Mistress?"

Alannah chooses to misinterpret him. Perhaps he'll take the hint and avoid the awkward conversation she now anticipates.

"I'm sure you'll see me around the scene, Simon. I usually see clients in private dungeons, but sometimes I go to public events. I often drop in to Pain when Richard's working there. I've been known to turn up at Torture Garden. And you can always come to my next ball."

He nods sadly, and Alannah believes for a moment she has done enough to dissuade him, until he asks again.

"Yes. But what I meant was, please can I serve you again Mistress?"

She sighs. This is the problem with the green ones. No idea of what is a reasonable expectation and what is a ridiculous fantasy.

"I'm sorry Simon but that's not going to happen. This was a one-off."

"Did I do something wrong?"

"No, Simon. You were a very good boy. I enjoyed you very much."

He gazes up at her with puppy dog eyes but holds his tongue. She rolls her eyes and concedes an explanation.

"My life is busy and complicated. We had fun, but you're not ready for someone like me, and I don't want any new commitments right now. Besides, you couldn't afford me."

"How much…"

"No, Simon. It's not going to happen. Let's not part on bad terms. Please stop asking."

He bites his lip, ego more bruised than his skin.

"Sorry, Mistress."

"Good boy. Perhaps this will cheer you up." She reaches into a drawer in the sideboard for one of her cards, sliding it across the table to him.

"My private number. Don't disclose it to anyone. Don't abuse the privilege or you will be blocked. I only take calls from numbers I recognise, so when you're in the car send me a text so I can save you as a contact."

"Thank you, Mistress. I will."

Simon looks at the card in confusion, then picks it up. She continues before he has a chance to ask a stupid question.

"For aftercare, Simon. You might feel strange over the next few days. Perhaps it's the brain re-calibrating the neurotransmitters after the flood created by the play session. Perhaps it's the social vacuum left after an intense connection is made and then broken. Perhaps you won't feel it at all. But if you do drop, if you feel low in the coming days and you need reassurance, or if you'd like to talk through what happened, you should call me. If I don't answer, leave a message and I'll call you back as soon as I can. Yes?"

"Yes, Mistress."

"If you fall hard, you might find it difficult to make the call. I want you to know that I expect you to phone. You don't have to, but I expect you to. You won't be interrupting anything because I will only answer if it's convenient.

I won't be annoyed, and you won't be a burden, so if you find yourself overthinking it then just call. Do you understand?"

"Yes, Mistress." His face wears a serious expression. He clutches the card with both hands.

They are interrupted by Sarah, returning with his belongings.

"Good boy. Now get dressed. You need to be ready when the car arrives."

Sarah places the folded clothes on the table, setting his shoes and bag on the floor nearby. She takes a step backwards and stands, waiting for the towel. The boy seems reluctant to strip in front of her, but after a moment's hesitation he stands up and begins to dress himself. Sarah takes the towel out of the room, presumably towards the laundry.

Richard strides in, bottle of wine in hand. He searches for the corkscrew in the sideboard and slides the cork out with a satisfying 'pop'. He pours three glasses of wine, setting the bottle on the table beside them. He glances at Simon, then smiles at Alannah.

"Elvis is on his way. Simon will be leaving us shortly. Is everything OK in the kitchen?"

Richard shakes his head.

"The food is good. Danny – less so. I think it's time to go back to the doctor. I'll call tomorrow and arrange an appointment."

As if summoned by the mention of his name, Danny walks in bearing a tray loaded with food. He gingerly places it on the table and unloads the contents onto the mats. Several dishes of vegetables, a pot of roast potatoes, homemade bread with oil and balsamic vinegar, and a perfect pie, steaming from the holes in its crisp crust and looking like it should be on the cover of a cookery book. Alannah inhales, savouring the aromas as her stomach growls.

Sarah returns too, carrying a jug of water which she pours into four glasses before setting it on the table. Finished, she takes her place behind her chair, and waits.

Danny is noticeably uncomfortable as he lays out their meal. He visibly twitches as he places the knives, one by the bread and another by the pie. He looks to his Master for reassurance.

"It's fine, Danny."

"I still think we shouldn't eat it, Master. I have a terrible feeling about it. Something bad got in it."

"I said, it's fine." Richard says firmly. "Stop worrying. You know how it works, Danny. You're mine. My boy. I'm the only bad thing that's going to happen to you. Everything else has to get through me first. Right?"

Danny's response is quiet, the whisper taking over his usual rasp.

"Right, Master. I'm sorry. Am I in trouble?"

"No. It's not your fault. You can't help it, so you won't be punished. But I do think we need to revisit your medication."

Danny looks at his feet and nods, as Richard picks up the bread knife and begins cutting slices from the loaf. He exchanges a concerned glance with Alannah. Danny's mental health was never good, but this is the worst she's seen him in months. No wonder Richard is worried.

Danny sidles to stand behind his chair, next to Sarah. Simon remains quiet at the far end of the table, the only one seated. He looks confused, but Alannah feels no pressure to offer an explanation. It's none of his business, and the car will be here soon anyway. Then she can finally eat. She takes another deep breath as the scent of warm bread rises over the meaty smell of pie.

With several slices of cut, Richard picks one up and tries to place it on his side plate.

"SARAH!"

Her head snaps up in fear.

"Master?"

"On which side of the setting do the side plates belong, Sarah?"

"On the left, Master." She looks desperately at the table. Her eyes widen as she realises her error. "Oh, shit."

"And where did you put them?"

"On the right. Sorry, Master."

"Fix it, then two on the board, Sarah. And you will eat your meal with your left arm behind your back, to help you remember."

"Thank you, Master." She scurries round the table, fixing the plates – Richard's first, then Alannah's unoccupied place, Danny's and finally her own. As she walks, bruises wobbling, Richard watches with a glint in his eye.

When the table is corrected she walks over to the blackboard on the wall, next to the two framed contracts. The side with Sarah's name is already busy with tally marks

– more than ten since Wednesday. Danny's side has only two marks. About normal for this point in the week, then. Sarah picks up the chalk and draws two more marks on her side. Alannah reflects on its new hanging place. The board is much more convenient here than downstairs in the dungeon, but it does mean they need to be more mindful of visitors.

"We mustn't forget to move those downstairs next week."

"She can't read them anyway," Richard replies. "Her eyes are worse than she'll admit."

"Yes, she's just as stubborn as her treasured perfect son."

Richard smiles, eyebrow arched, but before he can reply they are interrupted by Alannah's phone lighting up. A message from Elvis – the car is ready.

"Time to go, Simon."

"Yes, Mistress." He stands, throwing his bag onto his shoulder. As she leads him into the hallway, she calls back to Richard.

"Start without me, I'll be back soon."

The sound of scraping chairs indicates that he has told the slaves to sit. Alannah picks Simon's jacket from the coat hooks and hands it to him.

"Don't forget this. Are you all set?"

"Yes Mistress. Thank you, for everything. It was… incredible."

She moves towards the door, releasing the yale and swinging it open.

"You're welcome Simon. I had fun, and you did very

well. Elvis will take you home now. Don't forget to send that text."

"Yes, Mistress, I won't." Simon steps through the door, hesitates, and turns back. "Do you... do you live like this all the time?"

"Yes. Glorious isn't it?"

"I didn't know people could. I hope I meet someone who wants to live like that."

Alannah smiles, pleased that the fetish world has a new convert. "I'm sure you will, Simon, soon enough. You'll make someone a good little slave. Just start slowly and be careful to find someone who takes your safety seriously. OK?"

"Yes, I will. Goodbye Mistress."

"Goodbye Simon." She shuts the door. Only the glow from the fanlight above, radiating into the twilight, reveals that the house is occupied.

Simon turns and descends the dark steps, following the path down to the road beyond. The black Bentley is waiting, its rear door held open by the incongruous Elvis.

"Good evening, Sir. Where can I take you to tonight?"

Simon gives him the address and gets into the back of the car. Elvis closes the door and walks round to the driver's seat. The engine starts, and they pull away. Houses and streets stream past the blackened windows.

Simon pulls out his phone to text Mistress as instructed. He has two messages and a voicemail – all from Kate. He smiles. She'll be itching to hear the gossip, and he has a hell of a lot to tell. He crafts a careful message to Mistress – thinking of her already evokes bittersweet memories of excitement and rejection – then sends a message to Kate.

On my way home. Should be there in 20 mins. Wanna catch up?

The reply flashes up quickly.

I'm coming over now for a full debrief. I want to know EVERYTHING. I'll bring wine. Kate xx

Twenty-Seven

Bedtime

Two hours later, Sarah and Danny are clearing the plates from the table. Alannah is full of food and contentedly tired. The pie was delicious, even Danny had calmed down and agreed there was nothing bad in it after all. She eyes up the last few strawberries in the dessert bowl but decides against a second helping.

The slaves disappear with an arm load of dishes each. Richard looks pensive, nursing the remains of his wine over his empty bowl. She slides her foot under the table to rub his ankle.

"Still worried about Danny?"

He fixes her with a piercing gaze, then frowns and returns to contemplating his glass.

"He's losing his grip on reality again. He's already on a high dose, I'm not sure they can increase it. I don't know what else I can do for him."

"He'll come around. He feels secure with you. You can get through to him when he won't listen to anyone else. He's lucky to have you. You take such good care of him."

Richard smiles briefly. "It's kind of you to say so. But none of it matters if I can't keep him out of residential care. He won't cope in there. He'll lose his research post, and end up drugged out of his mind, if he doesn't manage to kill himself. And things are changing here. We are going to have other priorities. He's very observant. I think he's guessed."

"Already? What makes you think that?"

Richard tips his glass at her. "He can count."

"Even Sarah can count."

"Yes, but Sarah isn't writing a thesis on the interpretation of complex data."

She laughs wryly. "Well, they'll both know sooner or later. We need to talk about it first."

"We do. But not in the house. Can you do dinner on Thursday? I could book somewhere decent."

"Thursday works, but I'd rather not go upmarket. Let's just grab a burger somewhere."

"Frankies?"

"Perfect. It will have to be late though. Nine?"

"Nine it is. If you're coming straight from a client shall we meet there?"

"Yes, that works."

She smiles and slides her foot higher up her husband's leg, hooking her toes around the back of his calf. He arches one eyebrow at her.

"Come to bed?"

*

Richard follows his wife into his bedroom and shuts the door. As soon as it is closed, she steps into his arms and kisses him.

"Come to bed." She strips off her robe, dumping it on the floor and slides under the covers.

Richard grins and strips his own clothes as quickly as he can.

He lies down next to her on the mattress. She wastes no time wrapping herself around him and kissing him again.

"Looks like someone enjoyed herself today."

"Yes. Very much." She hooks a leg around his hip and begins to press against him, rubbing her clitoris along the length of his hardening cock.

He pushes back against her, moving slowly but firmly. "It shows."

"I gave him his first lesson in the crop. He made those little noises, the ones they can't hold in. The ones that let you know exactly how much they like the pain."

"I'm glad he was a good investment. He wasn't cheap." Richard pulls back and tries to slide downwards so he can get inside her, but she groans and tenses her leg to push him back against her clit.

"And then we had a second round with a violet wand."

"Did you now?" he rubs against her with growing fervour.

"Did you hear him scream when he came?"

Richard pauses, slowing the rhythm.

"You let him come?"

"Twice."

He exhales in displeasure. "God, woman, twice? You've spoilt him. He'll expect it every time now."

"Yes, but that's someone else problem."

"You're not going to see him again? I thought you liked him? Why not bring him back for another round. Hell, why not keep him? We've got the space, and he didn't seem like much trouble. Apart from those high expectations you've imprinted on him."

"No, I don't think so. The timing's off. He's too green, he'd be too much work to train. Once was enough. And anyway, if I did start something, you'd be trying to fuck him the whole time."

He shrugs. "Mmh, I won't deny it. But I'd let you watch?"

"No deal. I don't like sharing men. And the only person I want to fuck right now is you." She kisses him and finally relaxes her leg enough to let him slide inside the heat of her body. It makes him catch his breath, even now, after years together.

"Damn, you're wet. You really did like him. What got you like this?"

She closes her eyes and grinds her pelvis towards his, dragging him deeper inside.

"Oh, he tried so hard, bless him. He knew nothing, but he was very eager. He let me take him right up to his edges. There was one point when he was strapped to the bench... he was struggling with the pain, he was shouting and cursing and he kept lifting his head. His neck is so long, and his Adam's apple slid up and down every time he moaned. And all the time, I was thinking about blades and how beautiful his throat would look smeared in blood."

As she whispers, he feels the walls of her cunt tighten around him. She's not been this hot for ages. He likes it, seeing her this ravenous, but it's going to be over too soon.

"Slow down a little, let's enjoy it a while."

"No. No, I want it quick and hard. Don't stop, just fuck me."

How can he argue with that? If she wants it fast he will oblige, and push all of her buttons.

"If he's so keen to please he might agree to it. Next time, he might let you cut him? Don't you think you could persuade him?"

She arches her back in pleasure. "Mmh, you know, I think I could. But it's a terrible idea. He's too innocent to understand the risks. Consent would be borderline at best."

"Well, in that case, you should definitely invite him back. Give him a real happy ending, a permanent one that ends with him covered in gore. We'll slice him open together, drain him dry and fuck in a pool of his blood."

She wraps her leg higher around his waist, bucking into him with greater urgency.

"Mhhhh. Oh God, Richard, let me get on top."

He concedes his position as she slides over to straddle him. She rides him hard, mouth open and head thrown back, fast and desperate until she suddenly hits her orgasm, doubling forwards over him with a cry.

When she finally stops shuddering, she kisses his jaw and leans her nose against his, recommencing at a less demanding rhythm. After the overwhelming sensation of her furious desire, this new pace is frustratingly slow. His cock aches for more.

"Do you want to come too?"

"Yes," he growls, "Yes, I want to come." He doesn't wait for permission but unceremoniously flips her onto her back, resting his elbows either side and grabbing hold of her shoulders to give full leverage as he thrusts deep into her, shoving hard between her wide spread legs, pumping inside her until he, too, reaches orgasm.

Breathing hard, he softens his arms and picks a loose strand of hair from his mouth. After a moment, he slides out from her and settles down beside her. They lie together, legs entangled, enjoying the afterglow.

"You're a bad influence, you are."

"I am, woman, but you like it."

"I admit it, I do." She pauses. "You wouldn't really do it though. Would you? A blood play threesome with an unwilling victim?"

He meets her gaze for a moment, then shakes his head. "No. Not to say I wouldn't enjoy it. But it isn't right. No consent, no scene. Still, there's nothing wrong with a little fantasy, is there?"

"Nothing at all. It doesn't hurt anyone to enjoy the idea. It's just… sometimes I fear what would happen if you lost control of your urges."

"I don't. I have a longstanding agreement with my worse appetites. I feed him what he wants, and he stays under control. The alternative doesn't bear thinking about."

"Probably for the best. No vampire play for me, then."

"If anyone could persuade me, it's you. But we all have our limits. And blood play is so messy, just think of the clean up. Once was enough."

She grins broadly. "Oh, that was incredible. I'll never forget it. Every detail was perfect, you planned it so well."

"Mmh, not every detail. Getting arrested wasn't part of the plan."

"Oh, I don't know. It added a certain drama. And it worked, didn't it? I mean, I married you."

"You did, Mrs Donohue. Although I'm not sure I'll ever make an honest woman of you."

"Pot, kettle, my love."

"Well, that's as may be."

She giggles. He raises his eyebrow quizzically, and her gentle laugh bubbles deeper.

"Poor Mike. He was so confused."

"Poor Mike? I was the one in handcuffs. Not my way up at all!"

"Well it all worked out in the end."

"Yes, it did." He leans in to kiss her, two wet mouths languidly meeting in comfortable affection. They lie still for a while, bodies gently rising and falling as they breathe, growing drowsy together.

"You're sure you didn't want to fuck the slave?"

"I'm sure. If I wanted him I would have had him."

"OK. You were just so turned on. And…"

"and…what?"

"Well, sometimes I wonder if all that religious indoctrination affects you more than you think? You hardly ever have sex with other people now we're married."

"I don't think that's the reason. I get more out of the tease and denial than sex itself. There's something about PIV that feels vaguely submissive. It just doesn't feel right with a slave. And as long as I've got vanilla on tap from my desperately attractive husband, why would I want to go elsewhere?"

"As long as you're happy. No gilded cage, remember?"

"No gilded cage. And that goes both ways. If I was worried about you having more partners than me, I'd talk to you about it. So you can stop wallowing in your Catholic guilt, OK?"

"Oh, there's not much of that left. I got rid of the guilt when I got rid of the religion. If there is a God, why would he care about whose hole I stick my cock into, any more than about which bathroom I take a piss in?"

"Oh great, thanks. And you wonder why I'm not a fan of receiving penetration."

"I didn't mean you… damn."

"I know. It's OK, I'm winding you up. You're the exception to the rule."

"Well, no disrespect intended. Sorry. And… I'm sorry I was an asshole last week. About Danny."

She strokes a finger lazily across his chest.

"Thanks for saying so. I know the timing is lousy. We'll work something out. And anyway, I think we should fall out more often if Simon is the kind of apology I can expect."

"So you'll forgive me, then?"

"I forgive you. I have to really, I don't want to ride anyone else's cock so you appear to have the monopoly."

He smiles, and untangles his legs from hers.

"I love you."

"I love you too."

With a deep sigh he lets himself relax contentedly into sleep.

Epilogue

Alannah re-tightens the laces of her top. She wouldn't normally care how much she reveals, but it would be rude to upstage the bride. That's why she'd ordered a long skirt, past her knees, and picked out a pair of ankle boots with a small block heel instead of her habitual stilettos.

She checks the mirror one last time. Yes, the outfit is a good choice. Skin tight latex meets the fetish dress requested on the invite, and the suit like cut gives a formal air. The green colour brings out her eyes, and the black edged detail draws attention to her better curves, away from those which gravity and time are doing their best to erode. Later, at the reception, she will keep a lookout for potential clients. Scene weddings are a rare opportunity worth exploiting to the full.

A knock on the door is followed by a nervous voice.

"Mistress Alannah, may I come in?"

It won't do to let him believe she is waiting for him. She quickly opens her lipstick and pretends to reapply the black to her lips.

"Yes, Simon, come in."

Simon has changed since she last saw him. His beautiful long hair is gone. Closely cut at the back, a little more length on the top, but nothing worth her attention any more. His body has bulked up too, no doubt the result of some gym routine enforced by his fiancée. He looks good – or at least more conventionally attractive – but she finds him less interesting than before. Perhaps it's just that everything seems lacklustre these days.

He is dressed in leather bondage gear – black shorts attached to straps which circle each leg and reach down to his ankles. Bare feet, wrist cuffs and a chest harness. His neck is empty, waiting for the collar he will receive during the ceremony. He is a different man to the one he would have become if she had kept him. Perhaps everything would have been different if she had kept him. But it's no use being maudlin, not at a wedding. She forces the familiar fake smile and turns to face him.

"Mistress Alannah, thank you so much for doing this. I wasn't sure you'd come – I wasn't sure the phone number would still work."

"It's a pleasure, Simon. I'm honoured to be asked."

She puts the lid back on her lipstick and picks up the dog leash from the table. She clips the heavy chain to the steel circle in the middle of his chest.

"Are you sure you want to do this, Simon?"

He smiles, shy but confident. "Yes, Mistress Alannah, I'm sure. I love her."

"There's nothing more dangerous in the world than love, Simon. Well, as long as you're sure. Shall we go?"

"I'm sorry Mistress Alannah, but they're running late. About fifteen minutes. I'm afraid we'll have to wait. My Mistress sends her apologies."

She sighs. "That's the trouble with big weddings, I suppose. So much to orchestrate."

"What was your wedding like, Mistress?" He asks quietly, unsure whether the topic is safe.

"It was very small. Just the two of us, Mike, and his mother. He didn't want the slaves there. We were very happy."

"I'm so sorry, Mistress... about what happened..."

"Please don't, Simon," she snaps, "I don't want your pity."

The silence is frosty. She wonders if she spoke too harshly. It can't be undone now. None of it can.

After a moment, he picks up the conversation again. He really has matured, the Simon she knew would have stayed nervously quiet after that reprimand.

"How is Toby doing? And Sarah?"

"They're fine. He's very taken with her. And she's utterly devoted to him, of course. She's been a great help; I don't know what I'd have done without her."

"That's good. She's lucky that you took care of her. You didn't have to."

"I promised him."

Simon nods. This time the silence is more amiable, and it is Alannah that breaks it.

"To tell you the truth, sometimes I'm a little jealous. It's odd. I was never jealous with Richard. Not once."

"I know it's not my place, Mistress. But if there's anything I can do to help. Anything at all, even if it's something small."

Alannah closes her eyes to hide the tears gathering there. Why not allow herself this chance? God knows, they are rare enough.

She nods.

"Just tell me how you remember him. Tell me what he was like the night he bought you."

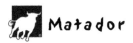